Hester

A Story Of Contemporary Life

Vol. II

by

Oliphant

Double9 BOOKS

Hester
A Story Of Contemporary Life
Vol. II
by Oliphant

ISBN: 978-93-70810-39-6

Published by

DOUBLE 9 BOOKS
2/13-B, Ansari Road
Daryaganj, New Delhi – 110002
info@double9books.com
www.double9books.com
Tel. 011-40042856

ABOUT THE AUTHOR

Margaret Oliphant was a Scottish author and historical writer who usually wrote under the name Mrs. Oliphant. She was born Margaret Oliphant Wilson on April 4, 1828, and died on June 20, 1897. She writes "domestic realism, the historical novel, and tales of the supernatural" as her short stories. Margaret Oliphant was born in Wallyford, near Musselburgh, East Lothian. She was the only daughter and youngest child still living of Margaret Oliphant (c. 1789–17 September 1854) and Francis W. Wilson, a clerk. We lived in Lasswade, Glasgow, and Liverpool when she was a child. In Wallyford, a street called Oliphant Gardens is named after her. As a girl, she was always trying new things with writing. Passages in the Life of Mrs. Margaret Maitland, her first book, came out in 1849. This was about the mostly successful Scottish Free Church movement, which was something her folks agreed with. Next came Caleb Field in 1851, the same year she met publisher William Blackwood in Edinburgh and was asked to write for Blackwood's Magazine. She did so for the rest of her life and wrote over 100 articles, including one that criticized Arthur Dimmesdale in Nathaniel Hawthorne's "The Scarlet Letter."

CONTENTS

CHAPTER I
THE YOUNG AND THE OLD 7

CHAPTER II
A FAMILY PARTY 16

CHAPTER III
CONFIDENCES 27

CHAPTER IV
ROLAND 35

CHAPTER V
WARNING 40

CHAPTER VI
DANCING TEAS 51

CHAPTER VII
THE FIRST OF THEM 62

CHAPTER VIII
A NEW COMPETITOR 74

CHAPTER IX
A DOUBLE MIND 86

CHAPTER X
STRAIGHTFORWARD 96

CHAPTER XI
A CENTRE OF LIFE 105

CHAPTER XII
WAS IT LOVE? 111

CHAPTER XIII
CHRISTMAS 118

CHAPTER XIV
THE PARTY AT THE GRANGE 132

CHAPTER I
THE YOUNG AND THE OLD

"I like your Roland," said Miss Vernon. She had come to pay one of her usual visits to her old relations. The grandson whom Hester had made acquaintance with without seeing his face, had now been nearly a week at the Vernonry and was known to everybody about. The captain's precautions had, of course, come to nothing. He had gone, as in duty bound, to pay his respects to the great lady who was his relation too, though in a far-off degree, and he had pleased her. Catherine thought of nothing less than of giving a great pleasure to her old friends by her praise. "He is full of news and information, which is a godsend to us country folks, and he is very good-looking, *qui ne gâte rien*."

Mrs. Morgan looked up from her place by the fireside with a smile of pleasure. She sat folding her peaceful old hands with an air of beatitude, which, notwithstanding her content, had not been upon her countenance before the young man's arrival.

"That is a great pleasure to me, Catherine—to know that you like him," said the old lady. "He seems to me all that, and kind besides."

"What I should have expected your grandson to be," said Catherine. "I want him to see the people here, and make a few acquaintances. I don't suppose that our little people at Redborough can be of much importance to a young man in town; still it is a pity to neglect an opportunity. He is coming to dine with me to-morrow—as I suppose he told you?"

The old lady nodded her head several times with the same soft smile of happiness.

"You are always good," she said; "you have done everything, Catherine, for me and my old man. But if you want to go straight to my heart you know the way lies through the children—my poor Katie's boys."

"I am glad that the direct route is so easy," Miss Vernon said in her fine, large, beneficent way; "at least in this case. The others I don't know."

Captain Morgan came and stood between his wife and the visitor. To be sure it was to the fire he went, by which he posted himself with his back to it, as is the right of every Englishman. His countenance wore a troubled look, very different from the happiness of his wife's. He stood like a barrier between them, a non-conductor intercepting the passage of genial sentiment.

"My dear Catherine," he said, with a little formality, "I don't wish to be unkind, nor to check your kindness; but you must recollect that though he is poor Katie's boy, she, poor soul, had nothing to do with the up-bringing of him, and that, in short, we know nothing about him. It has been my principle, as you know, of late years, to insist upon living my own life."

"All that, my kind old uncle, is understood," said Catherine. "There are a great many people, I believe, who are better than their principles, and you are one of them—that is all. I understand that you know nothing about him. You are only a man, which is a great drawback, but it is not to be helped: *we* know, though we have seen no more of him than you have. Isn't it so?"

She leaned forward a little, and looked across at the old lady, who smiled and nodded in return. Old Mrs. Morgan was not disturbed by her husband's disagreement. It did not even make her angry. She took it with perfect composure, beaming over her own discovery of her grandson, and the additional happiness it had brought.

"My old man," she said, "Catherine, has his own ways of thinking, we all know that; and sometimes he will act upon them, but most commonly not. One thing I know, he will never shut his doors on his own flesh and blood, nor deny his old wife what is her greatest pleasure—the thing that has been wanting to me all the time—all the time! I scarcely knew what it was. And if the boy had been distant or strange, or showed that he knew nothing about us, still I should have been content. I would have said, 'Let him go; you were right, Rowley, and not I.' But it is not so," the old lady went on after a pause, "there's love in him. I remember when the girls were married there was something I always seemed to want, I found out what it was when the first grandchild was born. It was to feel a baby in my arms again—that was what I wanted. I don't know, Catherine," she added with humility, "if you will think that foolish?"

"If I will understand—that is what you are doubtful of—for I am an old maid, and never had, so to speak, a baby in my arms; but I do understand," said Catherine, with a little moisture in her eyes. "Well, and this great handsome fellow, a man of the world, is he your baby that you wanted so much?"

"Pooh!" said the old captain. "The great advantage of being an old maid, as you say, is that you are above the prejudices of parentage. It is possible to get you to hear reason. Why should my life be overshadowed permanently by the action of another? That is what I ask. Why should I be responsible for one who is not me, nor of my mind?"

"Listen to him! You would think that was all he knows," said Mrs. Morgan; "there is no fathoming that old man, my dear."

"What I have to say is, that we know nothing of this young man," said the captain, shaking his shaggy head as if to shake off his wife's comments. "You will exercise your own judgment—but don't take him on mine, for I don't know him. He is well enough to look at; he has plenty to say for himself; I dare say he is clever enough. Form your own judgment and act upon that, but don't come and say it's our fault if he disappoints you—that is all I have to say. Excuse me, Catherine, if I take a walk even while you are here, for this puts me out—I allow it puts me out," Captain Morgan said.

"What has made him take this idea?" said Miss Vernon, when Captain Morgan had hobbled out.

"Oh, my dear, he has his fancies like another. We have had many things to put up with, and he thinks when it comes to the second generation—he thinks we have a right to peace and quiet in our old age."

"And so you have," said Catherine gravely, "so you have."

She did not ask any questions. Neither she nor any one knew what it was with which, in the other part of their lives, these old people had been compelled to "put up." Nor did the old lady say. She answered softly, "Yes, I think so too. Peace is sweet, but it is not life."

"Some people would say it was better."

"They never knew, those people, what life was. I like to see the children come and go—one here, one there. One in need of your sympathy, another of your help, another, oh Catherine, even that—of your pardon, my dear!" This made her pause, and brought, what was so unusual, a little glistening moisture to the old lady's eyes. She was silent for a moment, and smiled, perhaps to efface the impression she had made. "If you can do nothing else for them you can always do that," she said.

Catherine Vernon, who was sixty-five, and knew herself to be an old woman, looked at the other, who was over eighty, as a girl looks at her mother—wondering at her strange experiences, feeling herself a child in presence of a knowledge which is not hers. She had not experience enough to understand this philosophy. She looked for a little at her companion, wondering, and then she said, soothingly—

"We must not dwell upon painful subjects. This young fellow will not appeal to you so. What I like in him is his independence. He has his own opinion, and he expresses it freely. His society will be very good for my nephew Edward. If he has a fault—and, indeed, I don't think that boy has many—it is that he is diffident about his own opinion. Roland, if he stays long enough, will help to cure him of that. And how does the other affair go on?" she added, with a perceptible pause, and in a voice which was a little constrained. "No doubt there is great triumph next door."

Old Mrs. Morgan shook her head.

"It is curious what mistakes we all make," she said.

"Mistakes? Do you mean that I am mistaken about the triumph? Well, they have very good reason. I should triumph too, if having been turned out of a great house, like Mrs. John, I managed to get back again, and recover all that I had lost by means of a thing so entirely my own creation as a daughter. Even a son would have been different—I suppose. You know I am not a judge on that point," Catherine said with a laugh.

The old lady continued to shake her head slowly.

"The only one that has not made a mistake is Harry. If he could have got what he wanted, it would have been the best thing that could have happened. There is no complication about that. For him it would have been the best."

"Do you mean to say," said Catherine, her eyes lighting up with that fire of curiosity and interest which overcomes even the languor of age. "Do you mean to say that—he is not to get what he wishes? Oh, this is too much! That girl is eaten up with pride. What is she saving herself for, I wonder? What can she expect?"

Again old Mrs. Morgan shook her head, smiling softly as at blunders upon which she could not be too severe.

"I have said already what mistakes we make, Catherine! often in our own career, always about other people, my dear."

Upon this Catherine laughed, not having, though she esteemed her old relation greatly, as much respect for her judgment as probably it deserved. Miss Vernon was too sensible a woman either to feel or express any contempt for her own sex, as clever women who were not sensible used to do in those days; but there was an undertone in her mind of indifference, to say the least, of another woman's opinion. She had a feeling that it could not be any better, and most likely was not so good, as her own, for she had held a position not usual among women, and knew that not many would have proved equal to the emergency as she did. What the old captain said would have impressed her more than what his wife said, and this although she was perfectly aware that the old lady in many cases was considered the most judicious of the two.

"I know you are both fanatics for Hester," she said, "who is not my favourite as she is yours. You must take care that Roland does not fall a victim to her. There are few girls about, and in that case, when young men have a mind to make fools of themselves, there is no choice. Do not shake your kind head off; you know this is a thing in which we have agreed we shall never think alike."

"Never is a long day," said the old lady, tranquilly. She was well used to waiting. In her experience, so many things had come to pass which no one expected. Even now, she said to herself, if any one had told her that Roland Ashton would one day be under her roof—She added quietly, "You are too much alike to do each other justice."

At this Catherine grew red. It had been intimated to her before, and she had scarcely been able to support the imputation. But she mastered herself with an effort. Nowhere perhaps but in this house would she have done so; but these old people had an ascendency over her which she could not explain.

"We will say nothing on that point," she said, quickly. "Your news has taken me so completely by surprise. Are you sure of it? Why should Mrs. John's daughter have rejected so excellent a settlement? She is looking for something better, I suppose?"

"I think that was a mistake too," said the old lady. "She says herself that Harry, though he is not clever, is good and true. Ah! it is you who shake your head now. In some things even our Catherine fails; he is not the equal of Hester; but it is not my opinion that a man need be always superior to his wife. Where there is love, it does not matter. I should have been pleased to see it; but she is young; she thinks differently. She is looking for nothing consciously; but in her heart for love, which is the visitor one is always looking for when one is young."

"Pshaw!" said Catherine; "it is the old people that are romantic, not the young. It is the settlements that are the things to be considered; or perhaps she is thinking of a title? Her mother is capable of any nonsense," she said with a scornful laugh.

Mrs. Morgan made no reply. Her peaceful aspect with her folded hands, the soft little smile on her old mouth, the slight shake of the head, was perhaps a trial of patience for the other, who felt herself thrown back into the category of the young and superficial by this calm expectation and quietness. Catherine Vernon was still in the region of prejudice and dislike. She had not lived into that superior sphere of toleration and calm. Impatience filled her veins. But she mastered herself, the atmosphere subduing her. And Captain Morgan came hobbling back, having calmed himself down too.

"Ellen has come back," said Miss Vernon, to change the subject, "from Paris, with clothes enough for all the neighbourhood. It amuses me to think of her among the bonnet-shops. What true enjoyment! and scarcely less now to show them to all her friends. Now there is a pleasure you cannot enjoy, uncle. A man could not call his friends together to look at his new hats."

"There is no telling what a young man can do in the way of folly till he is put to it," said the captain. "I am loth to recognise any inferiority. What do you think about all these failures, Catherine? or rather, if you have withdrawn from it, what do the boys think?"

"I hope I am still capable of giving an opinion," said Miss Vernon. "None of them touch us, which is the chief thing. For my part, speculation in this wild way is my horror. If you could see the proposals that used to be put before me! Not an undertaking that was not the safest and the surest in the world! The boys are well indoctrinated in my opinions on that subject. They know better, I hope, than to snatch at a high percentage; and love the substance, the good honest capital, which I love. I think," she continued, "there is a little of a miser in me, or perhaps you will say in all women. I love to see my money—to count it over like the—— By the way, it was the king that did that while the queen was eating her bread and honey. That goes against my theory."

"A good many things go against your theory. They say that there are no such wild speculators as women. It seems easy to them that a sort of miracle should happen; that something should come out of nothing."

"They have not had my experience," said Catherine. "But Edward and Harry are as steady as two churches; that is," she added with a complacency which they all recollected afterwards, "Edward is the head; the other fortunately has the good sense not to attempt to think for himself."

"Hester would have done that for him," said Mrs. Morgan, in an undertone; but Catherine caught it and went on with heightened colour, for the idea that Hester—*that* girl!—might have had something to say in the government of the bank, struck her as if some one had given her a blow.

"Edward is the heart and soul of everything," she said. "How fortunate it was for me that my choice fell upon that boy. I should say he had an old head on young shoulders, but that I don't like the conjunction. He is young enough. He has always been accustomed to family life, and loves his home."

"It is, no doubt," said Captain Morgan, kindly, "that he has had the advantage of your own experience and teaching more than the other, Catherine."

"That would be a delightful thought for me," Miss Vernon said with a suffusion of pleasure in her eyes. "Perhaps there is some truth in it. I have done my best to share my lights, such as they are, with him; but he goes beyond me. And to think that I hesitated between Edward and Harry! I hope I am grateful to Providence that turned me to the best. The other family are following out their lot quite characteristically. Ellen's husband has a good deal of worldly sense, which is wanting to that bit of a butterfly. He is trying hard to get her to make up to me. She has come to see me twice, full of pretty speeches about Algy's great respect for me. Human nature," said Catherine with a laugh, "is as good, nay, far better, than a play. How cunning it thinks it is, but in reality how very easy to see through."

Here old Mrs. Morgan began to shake her head again, smiling always, but with an indulgent, gentle contradictoriness which was more near making Miss Vernon angry than anything she had encountered in this house before.

"What does she sit there for, like a Chinese idol?" said the captain. "She has a wonderful opinion of herself, that old woman. Human nature may be easy to see through, but it is very hard to understand, Catherine. What is that the Bible says about 'deceitful above all things'? When you try to get hold of yourself, did you ever find a more slippery customer? There's a kind of amusement in it, when you are up to all your own dodges."

"Rowley, my dear!" said the old lady, surprised.

"It is true I am too old for slang: but one picks it up, and sometimes it is happy enough. I say when you are up to your own dodges; but that is difficult, and takes a great deal of time. To find yourself trotting forth the same old pretences that you did at twenty, attempting to throw the same sort of dust in your own eyes, is wonderful. There is a sort of artlessness in the artifice that is amusing, as you say; but it is only amusing when you are strong enough to get the upper hand."

"When which of you gets the upper hand? for there seem to be two of you," said Catherine, not so much amused in her own person as she made a pretence of being—for this was certainly not her view.

"To be sure," said the old captain, "there are two of you, we all know that; and in most cases one of you a very silly fellow, taken in on every hand, while the other man sniggers in his sleeve. Of course I am speaking from my own side—ladies may be different from anything I know. But after all," he went on, "I don't think so; for I've been a woman myself, so to speak, through *her*, for sixty years—that is a long spell. I don't see much difference, though in some things she has got to the last word sooner than I."

"I think we mean different things," said Catherine, rising; "that was not the view I was taking. Yours is better in the moral aspect, for I suppose it is more profitable to judge ourselves than others; but one cannot always be studying one's self."

There was a half-apology in her tone, and at the same time a half-impatience. She did not desire to be turned from the comedy which she had in her way enjoyed for years, seeing through, as she said, all the little world of dependents that hung about her, drawing out their weaknesses, perceiving the bitter grudge that lay under their exterior of smiles, and the thousand ways in which they made up to themselves for the humiliation of being in her debt—in order to turn to what might prove the less amusing contemplation of her own weaknesses, or recognise the element of evil in that which was certainly not amusing. Her carriage was standing at the gate which admitted to the garden front of the Vernonry, and it was with a sense of comfort that she got rid of the old captain at his door, and threw a keen, half-laughing glance at the windows on the other side. Mr. Mildmay Vernon was making himself very uncomfortable at the only angle of his room which permitted him to see the gate, watching for her exit. He kissed his hand to her as she paused and looked round before getting into the carriage, and Catherine realised as if she had seen it, the snarl of mockery with which this salutation was accompanied. In the intervening space were the two sisters keeping the most vigilant watch for her reappearance, counting the minutes which she spent on the other side of the house, and saying ill-natured things to each other as they nodded and waved their hands. She was aware of the very tone in which these speeches would be made, as well as if she had heard them, and it gave her a great sense of enjoyment to reflect that they were all sitting in rooms well warmed and carefully kept, and full of benevolent prevision of all their wants, while they thus permitted themselves to sneer and snarl at the bestower. Just as she drove away, Hester by chance opened the verandah door, and came out to gather some of the leaves of the Virginia creeper which were dropping with every blast. Hester's serious eyes met hers with scarcely any greeting at all on either side. Catherine did not know very well how it was that this girl came into the comedy. Had she been Harry's betrothed, Miss Vernon could have understood it, and though she could not but have felt the triumph of her old rival, yet it would have added delightfully to the commonplace drama in which everybody pursued their own mean ends under high-sounding pretences. She would have been able to smile at the commonplace young fellow taken in by the delusion that he was loved for himself, and laugh in the conviction that Harry's was no deep affection to be wounded, but that he could quite well take care of himself, and that between these two it would be diamond cutting diamond. But the present state of affairs she did not understand. All that was amusing in it was the doubtless unbounded disappointment of the scheming little mother, who thus must find all her fine schemes collapsing in her hands. She could not refrain from mentioning the matter at dinner that evening, though Edward had a little failed on the former occasion, in that backing up of all her opinions and feelings which she had been accustomed to expect from him.

"I find there is to be no match such as that we were speaking of," she said. "Harry has either drawn back or he is refused. Perhaps it may be that he has thought better of it," she added suddenly, without premeditation, grudging, as perhaps was natural, to let her young antagonist carry off the honours of the day.

"I thought it was not quite so certain as people seemed to believe."

"Do you mean that Harry would persevere?"

"I mean that she would accept him, Aunt Catherine. She is not a girl, so far as I can judge, of whom one could ever be so sure."

"In the name of wonder," cried out Miss Vernon, "what does she expect? Good heavens! where is she to get another such chance again? To refuse Harry, for a girl in her position, is madness. Where does she think she will get another such offer? Upon my word," said Catherine, with a little laugh, "I can scarcely help being sorry for her poor little mother. Such a disappointment for Mrs. John—her White House and her recovered 'position' that she loves so dearly, and all her comforts—I could find it in my heart to be very sorry for her," she said, with another little laugh.

Edward gave a glance up at her from his plate, on which he had the air of being intent. The young man thought he saw through Catherine, as she thought she saw through all the other inmates of her little world. What he did see through was the superficial badness which her position had made, but he had not so much as a glimmering of the other Catherine, the nobler creature who stood behind; and though he smiled and assented, a sensation of disgust came into his heart. He, too, had his comedy of human nature, which secretly, under cover of his complacency and agreement with Catherine's opinion, he regarded with the bitterest and angriest scorn. What an extraordinary shock would it have been for his companion, who felt herself to sit in the place of the audience, seeing the puppets play their pranks upon the stage and exhibit all their fooleries, to know that she herself was the actor, turned outside in and seen through in all her devices, to this boy whom she loved!

CHAPTER II
A FAMILY PARTY

"A grandson of Captain Morgan! Well, that is not much to meet us at our wedding dinner—at least, if it is not our wedding dinner—Oh, I know there was our state one, and we met all the old fogies whom I detest!" cried Mrs. Algernon Merridew, born Ellen Vernon; "but this is only the second, and the second is quite as important as the first. She should have asked the county first, to introduce us properly—and then the town; but Aunt Catherine is one of the people who never do what's expected of them. Besides, I don't want to meet her relations on the other side. They're nobodies. She spends quantities of money upon them which she has no business to do, seeing it's the Vernons' money and not hers at all, if you come to that."

"Come, Nell," said her husband with a laugh. He was a dark young man, as was to be expected—seeing that she was so fair a young woman—good-looking, with whiskers, which were the fashion in those days, of a bushy blackness, and hair which suggested pomade. "Come, Nell," he said, "strike fair. Catherine Vernon does a great deal of good with her money, and doesn't spare upon the Vernons—all the town knows that."

"Oh no, she doesn't spare upon the Vernons—all those useless old creatures that she has up there in that horrid old-fashioned house! I think if she did a little more for real relations, and left those old fogies alone, it would be more like—— Expecting one to call upon them, and take all sorts of trouble! And look at poor old Harry kept with his nose at his desk for ever."

"Poor old Harry is very lucky, I think. Fair play is a jewel. If she doesn't do all you want, who do you expect would?"

"You, of course!" cried Ellen, as was natural: and they were so newly married that he thought it very pretty; "that is the good of you; and if you go in for Aunt Catherine too, when you know I can't endure her——"

"Of course the good of me is to do whatever you want," he said, with various honeymoon demonstrations; "but as for going in for Aunt Catherine—you must know this, Nelly, that I'm very proud of being connected with Catherine Vernon. I have heard of her all my life as a sort of goddess, you know. You must not put me off it all at once—I couldn't be put off it. There now, there's nothing to look sulky about."

"You are such an old Redborough person," Ellen said, with a little pout: which was very true. He was not, indeed, at all a good match for a Vernon; but his whiskers—things much admired in those days—and her self-will had worsted all opposition. He was no more than the son of the perfectly respectable and very well-to-do solicitor, who was universally respected in Redborough, and though Algernon had been in town and sown his wild oats, he had never entirely got out of his mind the instinctive conviction that Redborough was the centre of the world; and to feel himself within the charmed circle in which Catherine Vernon moved was a promotion which was intoxicating to the young man. Not even his devotion to his pretty wife, which was great, could bring him to disown that allegiance to Catherine Vernon which every Redborough man was born with. It was a sort of still more intoxicating proof of the dignity he had come to, that the pretty wife herself turned up her little nose at Catherine. That Mrs. Algernon should be so familiar with the highest excellence known to them, as to venture to do this, was to the whole family of the Merridews an admiration—just as a family entirely loyal might be flattered by having a princess among them who should permit herself to laugh at the majesty of the king; but this did not shake their own fidelity. And Algernon, though he ventured with bated breath to say "Aunt Catherine" when he spoke of her in his own family, had not got over his veneration for Miss Vernon. He had taken her in to dinner on the occasion of the great banquet, which Ellen described so lightly, with a sensation bordering upon the hysterical. Rapture, and pride, and panic were in it. He did not know, according to the vulgar description, whether he were on his head or his heels, and his voice made a buzzing in his own ears as he talked. The second time was to be in the intimacy of the domestic circle—if it had been to meet a crossing-sweeper it would still have been a bewildering gratification; but all the more, his wife's criticism and her indifference, and even discontent with the notice which to him seemed so overpowering an honour, pleased the young man. She felt herself every bit as good as Catherine, and yet she was his—Mrs. Algernon Merridew! The thought was one adapted to make his head swim with pride and delight.

It was entirely a family party, as Catherine had said, and a very small one. The Miss Vernon-Ridgways had been invited, to make the number even, and their preparations for the unusual honour had taken up four days at least. When they sailed into the drawing-room at the Grange, having spent ten minutes in shaking out the flounces and arranging the flowers and ribbons with which they were ornamented, it would be impossible to attempt to describe the disgust of the bride. She turned her eyes upon her husband, who for his part was in a state of beatitude not to be disturbed by trifles, with a look of indignant rage which he did not understand. "To think she should ask those old things to meet *us!* I declare I have a great mind to go right away," she whispered to Harry, who was more sympathetic. Harry allowed that it was almost beyond bearing. "But I wouldn't make a quarrel if I were you," he said. In the meantime the sisters went up beaming to their dear Catherine, whom they kissed with devotion. How well she was looking! how becoming her dress was! but that lovely lace would be becoming to any one! they cried. Catherine received all these compliments with a smile, and she took great pleasure in Ellen's disgust, and the way in which she turned her ear instead of her cheek to the salutations of the cousins, who were rapturous in their admiration of her in all her bridal finery. The entry of the stranger, who was unknown to any of them, made a diversion. Roland Ashton, when he was visible in the full light of Miss Vernon's drawing-room, turned out, in appearance at least, a very valuable addition to the society. Ellen, who was critical, and inclined by nature to a poor opinion of old Captain Morgan's grandson, looked at him with astonished, and indeed reluctant, approval. His whiskers were not so thick or so black as Algernon's; but he had a fine mass of dark hair, wavy, and rather longer than is now permitted by fashion, fine features and dark eyes, with a paleness which was considered very interesting in those days. He was much taller and of more imposing aspect than Edward, whose stature was not great; he was far more intellectual than Harry; altogether of the four young men present, his was no doubt the most noticeable figure. They all appraised him mentally as he came in—Catherine first of all, with a sensation of pride that the one individual who was her relation, without being the relation of her family, was a creditable novelty to introduce among them; the others, with various degrees of quickened curiosity and grudging. The grudge was intensified in the persons of the sisters, who could not endure this interloper. They had felt it their duty to draw the line at the Morgans long ago, and it was all they could do to behave with propriety at Catherine's table when they were seated beside the descendant of the old people on whom Catherine spent her money in what they felt to be an entirely unjustifiable way. They were the only persons present who kept up their grudge to the end. In Ellen's case it disappeared with the clear perception of his good looks. But when Mr. Ashton offered his arm to Miss Matilda Vernon-Ridgway, the look with which she received the offered courtesy was enough to freeze any adventurous young man into stone. It did not, however. It made him all but laugh as he glanced at Catherine, who for her part contemplated her cousins with much gratification. Miss Matilda placed the end of her finger upon the young man's arm. She kept at as great a distance as possible as she crossed the hall by his side. To the little speech about the weather, which he thought it his duty to make her, she returned a sort of inarticulate reply—a monosyllable, but conveying no meaning. When she was seated at table she flung herself, so to speak, upon her neighbour at the other side, who, as it happened, was Harry Vernon, and who was not prepared for the honour. All this was to Catherine as good as a play.

"What a climate, and what a poky old place this Redborough is," said Ellen, preparing to lead the conversation, as she finished her soup. She spoke apparently to Edward, but in reality to the company, which was not too large for general conversation. "It is dreadful to come back here in the beginning of winter from Abroad. I declare I quite envy you, you people who have never been Abroad; you don't know the difference. Bright sunshine all day long, and bands playing, and the best of music, and all your friends to talk to, sitting out under the trees. Compare that with Redborough, where, beyond a few tiresome little dinner parties, and perhaps three dances at Christmas——"

"The White House used to be a great addition to the cheerfulness of the place," said Edward. "Harry will have no heart to keep it up by himself now you have left him."

"Oh, Harry shall marry," said Ellen, "I have made up my mind to that; and as soon as we have got quite settled, I mean to set things a-going. I mean to have a Thursday, Aunt Catherine. We shall be glad if you'll come. It is to be a *Thé Dansante*, which is quite a novelty here. You learn so much better about all these things Abroad."

"Where is Abroad?" said Roland, in an undertone which was so confidential and intimate, that had he been anybody else, Miss Matilda must have yielded to its seduction. As it was, she only gave him a look of surprise at his ignorance, and cleared her throat and shook her bracelets in order to be able to strike in.

"A *Thé Dansante* is exactly the kind of entertainment that suits me," Catherine said.

"Yes, won't it be nice?" said Ellen, unconscious. "I learnt all the figures of the *cotillion*, which is the most amusing thing to end up with, and I made Algy learn it. As soon as ever our house is ready we shall start. It will be a new feature in society. As for Harry, till he's married he'll have to be content with bachelor's dinners, for I can't always be leaving Algy to look after him."

Here Harry murmured something, stammering, and with a blush, to the intent that the bachelor's dinners would last a long time.

"We don't see you so often at our place as we used to do, Mr. Harry," said Miss Matilda, sweetly. "It used to be quite a pleasure to watch for you; and the summer evenings were so tempting, weren't they? Oh, fie! it is very naughty to love and to ride away. We always said that was what was likely to happen, didn't we?" she said to her sister, on the other side of the table.

Miss Martha nodded and smiled in return, and cried—

"Oh, always," in a shriller tone.

"What's that you thought likely to happen? Then it didn't happen if it was Harry," cried Ellen, instinctively, ranging herself on her brother's side.

"But about this *cotillion*?" said Edward. "What is it? I thought it had something to say to a lady's dress. I am sure it had in the eighteenth century. We shall have to go to school to learn what your novelty means."

"She put me to school, I can tell you," cried Algernon, from the other end of the table. "I had to work! She is the most dreadful little tyrant, though she looks so soft."

"Dancing is neglected shamefully nowadays," said Miss Matilda; "shamefully! We were taught very differently. Don't you remember, dear, Mousheer D'Egmont and his little violin, Martha? we were taught the minuet first on account of our curtseys——"

"Oh, the funny, old-fashioned thing! You *never* curtsey nowadays; even in the Lancers it is only a bob," said Ellen, "or a bend mostly with your head. You never see such a thing nowadays."

"My dear! In the presence of your sovereign," said Miss Matilda, with dignity, "it *always* continues necessary. There is no change in that respect so far as I am aware, Martha, is there? You were in the habit of attending Drawing-rooms longer than I."

"Oh, never any change in that!" cried Miss Martha, rising upon herself, so to speak, and erecting her head as she looked from one end of the table to another. It was not often that they had such a triumph. They had been Presented. They had made their curtseys to their Sovereign, as Miss Matilda said.

Silence fell upon the table, only broken by the jingle of Ellen's bracelets, which she pushed up her arm in her mortification; and there were so many of them that they made a considerable noise. Even she was cowed for the moment; and what was worse was, that her husband being simple-minded, and getting a little familiar with Catherine, now turned his looks of awe and veneration upon the Miss Vernon-Ridgways, who were so well acquainted with the court and its ways.

And Catherine laughed.

"We are all behind in that respect," she said. "I am fond of pomp and ceremonial for my part. It is a pretty thing, but I like it best at a distance. It is my fault, I have no doubt, that your wife is ignorant of Drawing-rooms, Mr. Merridew."

"I always said so, Aunt Catherine," cried Ellen, who was ready to cry, in the midst of her triumph. "It is horrid for girls to have relations with those out-of-the-way notions."

Catherine only laughed; it was her habitual comment. She turned smiling to young Ashton by her side.

"You ought not to dislike state," he said, in an undertone; "you who are a kind of queen yourself—or, shall I say, grand duchess—in your own town?"

"A queen without any subjects," said Catherine, shaking her head. This time she did not laugh, and there was even a little glimmer of sadness in her eyes.

"Not so. I am a stranger, you know. When I go about the town, I hear of nothing but Catherine Vernon. They call you so, do you know—*tout court*, without miss or madam—that has a great effect upon one's imagination."

Young Merridew had thrust forward his head, and was listening, which perhaps was not very good manners.

"It is quite true," he said eagerly. "Ellen says I am a very Redborough person. I have been born and bred here. I can't remember the time when I didn't look up to—her, as if she was something above the human——"

"And yet you have married a Vernon!" said Catherine; but she was pleased. "It is not an uncommon thing in this world," she said. "People at a distance think more kindly of one than those who are near; but this is not talk for a dinner-table. Not to interfere with Ellen's *cotillion*" she said, in a louder tone, "I am thinking of a party for Christmas, young people. As it is for you, you must lay your heads together, and decide what it is to be."

Then there arose a flutter of talk, chiefly maintained by the ladies, but in which young Merridew was appealed to by his wife; and Harry, stimulated by the same hand, and Edward, mindful of his duties, took part.

Catherine and her young relative were left, as it were, alone, amid the babble of tongues.

"I cannot allow myself to look at it gravely," she said. "I laugh; it is the best way. They all take what they can get, but their opinions, if they were individually weighed, of Catherine Vernon, would surprise you. They don't think much of me. I dare say I quite deserve it," she said, after a pause, with another laugh. "Don't you think that in most cases enthusiasm is confined to those people who personally know the least of the object of it? That's an awkward sentence, but never mind."

"Isn't it the same thing as to say that a great man is never a hero to his valet, or that a prophet has no honour in his own country?"

"Not the last, at least," said Catherine; "for being no prophet, you yourself say I have got some honour in my country. As for the valet, I don't know," she continued, "but a maid, though she appraises you at your true value, and is convinced you are a fool in many things, still is not without a prejudice in your favour. She would like, though she maintains her erect position, to see the rest of the world bow down before you. That is amusing too."

"You are a philosopher," said the stranger, looking at her with a tender regard in his eyes, which made a great impression generally upon younger women, and moved even Catherine as with a sense of kindness—of kindness disproportioned to their actual knowledge of each other, which is a thing which conciliates everybody, looking as if it implied a particular attraction.

"Your grandfather thinks me a cynic," she said. She liked these few words of quiet talk in the midst of the mingled voices of the others, and was grateful to the young man who looked so sympathetic. "I don't know that I am a cynic, but rather than cry, I prefer to laugh. Is that cynicism?" He gave her a look which would have no doubt had a great effect upon the heart of a younger woman, and which pleased Catherine, old as she was.

"I think it is true philosophy; but some of us have feelings that will not be laughed at," said Roland. He was accustomed to make great use of his fine eyes, and on this occasion he did so with the greatest effect. There could not have been more tender sympathy than was in them. Could he be really so much impressed by her character and position, and the failure of true gratitude and kindness? Catherine Vernon would probably have laughed at any one else of her own age who had been so easily persuaded; but it is always so much more easy to believe in the sincerity of affection which is called forth by one's self! Her eyes softened as she looked at him.

"I think you and I, Roland, are going to be great friends," she said, and then turned with a slight little sigh, so small as to be almost imperceptible, to the louder voices appealing to her. "You must settle it among you," she said. "I give Edward *carte blanche*. The only thing is that it must take in everybody, all the Vernonry and our neighbours as well—a real Christmas party."

"Oh, don't you think, Aunt Catherine, Christmas is such a bore!" said Ellen, "and family parties! Let us have strangers. Let us have people we never set eyes on before. Christmas is so vulgar! Look at all the newspapers with their little stories; the snow on the ground and the wanderer coming home, and so forth. I am so glad we haven't got a wanderer to come home."

"Christmas brings a great many duties I am sure," said Miss Matilda. "Have you seen the charity flannel at Roby's, Catherine? It is so good, almost good enough to wear one's self; and the blankets really look like blankets, not horse-cloths. Do you think that is good or bad? What you give in charity ought to be different, don't you think? not to let them suppose they have a right—"

"You forget," said her sister, eager to get in a word, "that dear Catherine always gives the best."

"Ah! it is well to be Catherine," said Miss Matilda, "but many people think there should be a difference. What do you think, Mr. Harry? Catherine may consider poor people's feelings; but there are some who think it is wrong to do so—for who is like Catherine? She is always giving. She is always so considerate. Whatever she does is sure to be the best way."

"I am certain," said Algernon Merridew beaming with honest loyalty from where he sat by Miss Vernon's side, "that all Redborough is of that opinion; and Redborough ought to know."

"You mean all but the people to whom I give," said Catherine, "there are not so many of them: but they are the best judges of all, and I don't think they approve."

"There's nobody so unreasonable as the poor," said Ellen, "they are never satisfied. You should just see them turning over the pieces from my kitchen. Of course all the pieces are quite nice; everything is, I hope, where I am housekeeper. Oh, I know I am extravagant, I like the best of everything; but nothing satisfies the poor. Cold potatoes now with mayonnaise sauce are what I adore, but *they* throw them away."

"Perhaps they don't have the mayonnaise sauce?" suggested Edward.

"Oh, goodness! I hope not; that would be simply immoral," cried Miss Matilda. "But, Mr. Harry, you don't give your opinion, none of the gentlemen give their opinion. Perhaps that is because money is what they give, and one shilling is just like another. You can't have charity shillings. Oh, but I approve of charity flannel; and some people always like to make a difference in what they give to the poor. Poor ladies and gentlemen soon find that out, I assure you. People give you useful presents. If they want to invite you, they invite you when there's nobody there. They think a family dinner or high tea quite treat enough for you. And quite right, don't you think, when one is in the position of a dependent? It keeps people in their proper places. Dear Catherine buys the best flannel, better than I can afford, for her Christmas gifts. She is never like other people, always more liberal; but I should buy the whitey-brown, that is, if I could afford any at all you know."

"Don't attack me, Matilda," said Catherine, with a laugh, "all along the line."

"Oh, attack! *you*, dear Catherine? not for the world. We all know what a friend you are. What should we do without you? Whether we are in Paris fashions or our old silks, don't we owe it all to you?"

There was a little pause round the table which was somewhat awkward; for what could anybody say? The clever ones were all non-plussed, but Harry, who was the stolid one, suddenly became audible with his round rolling bass voice. "Whoever says that, and whether it was well meant or not, I say the same. It's all quite true. We owe everything to Aunt Catherine. I am always ready to say so, wherever I go."

"Have we come to Christmas toasts already?" said Edward intervening. "We had better not start that sort of thing before the time. We all know what we owe to Aunt Catherine."

"Hush, hush," she cried, waving her hand to him as she rose. "Now we shall release your noble intellects from the necessity of coming down to our level," Catherine said as she followed carefully Miss Matilda's long train. It was very long, though it was rather flimsy, and the progress of the ladies was impeded by it. Ellen swept out lightly in advance with a perfect command of hers. It was the first time she had preceded the old cousins in her dignity as a married woman, and the ring of her bracelets sounded like a little trumpet-note. As she followed them out Catherine Vernon returned to her habitual mood of amused indulgence. She had been almost sentimental for a moment, she said to herself, beguiled by that boy's sympathetic eyes, which no doubt he must make great use of among the young ones. She laughed at herself not unpleasantly, to think of the confidences she had almost been beguiled into. But it pleased her to think that it was her mother's blood which had exercised this influence upon her. After all, it might be the Vernons only who were sordid and ungrateful. The old captain and his wife had always been exceptions to her sweeping judgment of human nature. And now it was their descendant who had touched her heart. Perhaps it was only the Vernonry after all. But she was fully restored to her usual kind of amusement as she watched the progress of her three companions into a temporary but eager intimacy on the score of Ellen's Paris fashions which they were eager to examine. The bride was as eager to exhibit as they were to see, and was so well pleased with herself as to be impervious to the little covert blows which Miss Matilda gave under the shield of her flatteries. Catherine Vernon established herself in her own chair, and gathered her costly silken skirts about her, and took up the newspaper, which people in the country have to read in the evening instead of the morning; but she did not read much. She was diverted by the talk. "Crinoline is certainly going out," said Ellen. "I heard it from the very best shops. Look at mine, it is quite small, hardly to be called crinoline at all. This is the very newest, from the Grangd Magaseens du Louvre. You see yours are twice as big," Ellen added, making a little pirouette to exhibit the diminished proportions of her hoops. The Miss Vernon-Ridgways looked down upon their own skirts with unquiet eyes.

"The French are always so exaggerated," said Miss Matilda. "Ignorant persons have such strange ideas. They think really nice people in England take their fashions straight out of Paris, but that is quite a mistake. It has always to be modified by English good taste——"

Ellen interrupted with a little shriek. "Oh, good taste! You should just hear how they speak of that Abroad. Sometimes I could have cried. They say no woman knows how to dress herself in England. And when I come back and see the dreadful things that are worn here—— This is pretty," Ellen continued, drawing attention to a portion of her dress. "The Empress wore one just the same at a ball."

"Dear Ellen," said Miss Matilda, "and you wear it at a little family party! that shows the difference. I am sure it was done just to please us, to let us see what the new fashions are, in your unselfish way, dear!"

And Catherine laughed behind the newspaper. The honours of the occasion were to the old sisters after all.

In the meantime conversation of much more serious import, though scarcely more elevated, was going on round the table in the dining-room, where young Ashton had got the lead, though none of the others looked upon him with over-favourable eyes. There was no doubt that he was a very handsome fellow, and both Harry and Edward had that instinctive sense that he was a competitor likely to put them on their mettle, which is supposed to influence the bosoms of women alone. They thought (instinctively, and each in their different ways,) that he must be a coxcomb. They divined that he was the sort of fellow whom women admired, and scorned him for it—as women perhaps now and then indulge in a little sneer at a gentleman's beauty. But by and by he touched a chord which vibrated more or less in all their bosoms. He began to talk of the city, for which country men of business have a natural reverence. He revealed to them that he himself was on the Stock Exchange, and incidentally let fall an anecdote here and there, of the marvellous incidents, the fairy tales of commerce, that were taking place in those magic regions every day: of men who woke in the morning with the most moderate means at their command, and before night were millionaires. They gathered close about him as he added anecdote to anecdote. Edward Vernon was like tinder, prepared for the fire; for all his thoughts for some time past had been directed in that way. And young Merridew was launching forth upon life, rather more lavishly than was consistent with his income and prospects. Harry was the least interested of the three, but even to him the idea of making a fortune in a few hours and being able to retire to the country to give himself up to dogs and horses, instead of going down to the bank every morning, was a beatific suggestion. The present writer does not pretend to be able to inform the reader exactly how it was, or in favour of which schemes, that the poet of the Stock Exchange managed to influence these rustic imaginations, but he did so. He filled their minds with an impatience of their own slow business and its mild percentages, even when he seemed to praise it.

"Perhaps it does feel slow work; I can't say. I think it is a vast deal more wholesome. It is very hard to keep your head steady, you know, when you feel that the chances of an hour or two may make you the richest man in England."

"Or the poorest perhaps?" said Edward, more with the idea of subduing himself than checking this flow of instruction.

"Ye-es," said Ashton, indifferently, "no doubt that's on the cards: but it ought not to be if your broker has a head on his shoulders. About the worst that can happen, if you take proper precautions, is that you're no worse than you were to start with, and better luck next time. I don't approve the 'gain or lose it all' system. But what will Miss Vernon say if we stay here talking shop all the evening?" he added.

There was never a more clever conclusion; it was like the exciting close of an act in the theatre, for he could not be persuaded to begin again. When they went reluctantly into the drawing-room, Ellen thought her Algernon had taken too much wine; and even Edward, who never offended the proprieties in any way, had a curious light in his eyes, and did not hear when he was spoken to. But Catherine Vernon, for her part, did not notice anything except the filial kindness of young Roland, and the sympathy and understanding which shone in his eyes.

CHAPTER III
CONFIDENCES

"I would not speculate if I were you," said Ashton. "What would be the good? You are very well off as you are. You are making your fortune steadily, far better than if you did it by a successful *coup*. Yes, yes, I can understand that a man should desire a little more excitement, and rebel against the monotony of a quiet life, but not you, Vernon, if you'll excuse my saying so. You don't go in for any sort of illegitimate pursuit. You don't play or bet; you have no claim upon you that you want extraordinary means of supplying— —"

"How can you tell all that?" said Edward Vernon. "Do you think life's so easy a business that you can read it off from the surface, and make sure that everything is as it seems?"

"I don't say that. Of course, I go upon appearances. I can understand that perhaps you are tired of it— —"

"Tired of it!" He twirled his stick violently in his hand, hitting at the rusty bramble branches and gorse bushes that bordered the Common as if they were his enemies. "I suppose one is apt to tire of anything that lasts and never varies," he cried with a forced laugh. "Yes, I am tired of it. Quiet life and safe business, and the hope of making a fortune, as you call it, steadily, in twenty or thirty years— —Good life! Twenty or thirty years! Only think of the number of days in that, one after the other, one exactly like the other. I begin to feel as if I should welcome anything to break the monotony—crime itself."

"That means, old fellow," said Ashton, soothingly, "nerves, and nothing more."

Edward laughed out, a laugh which was not harmonious with the soft dulness of the autumnal atmosphere. "I have no nerves, nor tastes nor inclinations, nor any mind of my own," he said. "I do what it is the right thing to do. Though I am sick of it, I never show that. Nobody here has the slightest idea that I was ever impatient or irritable or weary in my life."

Ashton looked at him with some curiosity, but took no further notice. "Does Miss Vernon," he said, "take any share in the business of the bank—I mean, in the work, in the regulations?"

"Miss Vernon," said Edward, "takes a share in everything that is going on around her, it does not matter what. She has been so long used to be at the head of everything, that she thinks it her natural place; and, as she is old and a woman, it stands to reason— —"

"But she is a very intelligent woman; and she must have a great deal of experience."

"The experience of a little country town, and of steady business, as you call it—oh, she has all that. But put your own views before her, or suggest even the advantages of the circulation of money, quick turning over, and balance of losses and gains— —"

"I can understand that," said Ashton, "You don't appreciate the benefits of the Conservative element, Vernon. But for you and your steady-going banks, how could we operate at all? The money must be somewhere. We can't play with counters only in this game."

"There was no question of counters," said Edward; "we have the money in our hands. It seems to me that you and I should change places: you to do the steady business here, and please Aunt Catherine—who has taken a great fancy to you, you must know—I, to watch the tide, how it comes and how it goes."

"There might be worse arrangements," Ashton said with a laugh: but he added quickly, meeting a keen, sudden glance from Edward, "if you could transfer to me your training, and I mine to you. I am counted rather bold sometimes, you must know," he added, after a moment, returning that look. They talked with great apparent readiness and openness, but with a curious dread of mutual observation going on under the current of their talk all the time.

"So much the better," said Edward, "so long as you know when to hold in."

They were going along the side of the Common between the Grange and the Vernonry. It was Sunday afternoon—a dull day, the sky hanging low, the green parts of the Common very green, glistening with wetness, the gorse and brushwood very brown and faded. Nobody was about on this day of leisure. Even the slow country cart, the farmer's shandry, the occasional roll of a carriage, was absent from the silent road. There were no nursemaids and children from Redborough picking their way along the side path. Captain Morgan, feeling his rheumatism, had retired to his chimney corner; the young men had it all to themselves. Ashton had been lunching at the Grange. He was on the eve of going back to town to business, from which he declared he had been absent far too long. The object of his visit was not very clear to any one: he had left his grandparents for years without showing so much interest in them. But, whatever his motive had been, his expedition had not been without fruit. He had discovered a new and wealthy vein well worth working, and lit a fire which, no doubt, would light up still further illuminations, in some inflammable spirits. No one had received him more warmly than Edward Vernon, but he was less easy to make out than the others. He was less simple; his life did not correspond with the betrayals of his conversation, whereas neither Harry Vernon nor his brother-in-law, had anything to betray. What was evident, at least, was that Catherine Vernon smiled upon the acquaintance which had been formed so rapidly between her nephew and the stranger. She called Edward "your cousin" to Ashton, then laughed and apologised, explaining that where there were so many cousins it was difficult to remember that her relation was not Edward's too. When Ashton replied, "There is connection enough to justify the name, if it is agreeable to Vernon," there could be no doubt that it was, at least, agreeable to her. She smiled upon them from her window as they went out together, waving her hand. And no foolish mother could have been more unaware than Catherine, that the knowledge that she was there, watching with tender looks of affection the two figures as they went along, was to Edward irksome beyond expression. He felt no charm of love in the look, but substituted suspicion for tenderness, and believed that she was watching them, keeping them in sight as far as her eyes could carry, to spy out all they did, and make for herself an explanation of every gesture. He would not even have twirled his stick and cut down the brambles but in a momentary fit of forgetfulness. When they got beyond her range, he breathed more freely, but, even then, was not without a recollection that she had her opera-glasses at hand, and might, through them, be watching his demeanour still.

"Let us go this way," he said, turning into the road, which slanted away on the nearer side of the Vernonry, leading out into the open country and brown fields.

Ashton hesitated a moment. "I am not sure that I am not expected at home. It is my last day," he said.

"Home is a kind of irons," said Edward, "hand-cuffs, ankle chains. One is always like an unhappy cockatoo on a perch. Any little attempt at flight is always pulled back."

"I don't think that is my experience. My old people are very indulgent; but then, I am a mere visitor. Home does not mean much to me," said Ashton. If he had been in the presence of any lady he would have sighed as he said this—being in absolute freedom with one of his own kind he smiled, and it was Edward who sighed.

"There is such a thing as having too much of it," he said. "What I suffer from is want of air. Don't you perceive it? There is no atmosphere; every breath has been breathed over and over again. We want ventilation. We welcome every horror with delight in consequence—a murder—or even a big bankruptcy. I suppose that is why bankruptcies are so common," he added, as if struck with the idea. "A man requires a great deal of original impulse before he will go the length of murder. The other has a milder but similar attraction; you ruin other people, which shakes them up, and gives a change of air."

"Ill-omened words," said Ashton, laughing, and throwing out the fore-finger and little finger of his right hand with a play at superstition. "Ugly at all times, but especially when we are talking of business and the Stock Exchange."

"Are you aware," said Edward, sinking his voice, "that our predecessor, before Aunt Catherine, did something of the kind?"

"Who was he?"

"A certain John Vernon. His wife lives yonder, with the rest of Aunt Catherine's dependents in that red house. He found it too much for him; but it was a poor sort of a flash in the pan, and hurt nobody but himself."

"You would like to do more than that," said Ashton, with a laugh.

But in Edward's face there was no jest.

"I should like," he said, "if I broke down, to carry the whole concern along with me. I should like to pull it down about their ears as Samson pulled the temple, you know, upon his persecutors."

"Vernon," said Roland, "do you know that you are very rash, opening out like this to me? Don't you see it is quite possible I might betray you? I have no right to preach, but surely you can't have any reason to be so bitter. You seem tremendously well off, I can tell you, to a friendless fellow like me."

"I am very well off," said Edward, with a smile; "no man was ever better. I came out of a struggling family where I was to have gone to the colonies or something. My next brother got that chance, and here I am. John Vernon, so far as I can hear, was an extravagant fool. I have not the least sympathy with that. Money's a great power, but as for fine houses, or fine furniture, or show or dash as they call it——"

"I told you," said Ashton, "you have no vice."

Edward gave him a dark, suspicious look.

"I have even a contempt for it," he said.

"There are plenty of men who have that—a horror even; and yet can't do without the excitement."

"I prefer your sort of excitement. John Vernon, as I say, was a fool. He ran away, poor wretch, and Catherine stepped in, and re-made everything, and covered him with contempt."

"He is the father (is he dead?) of the—young lady—who is such a favourite with my grandfather?"

"Hester? Oh, you know her, do you? One of Aunt Catherine's pensioners in the Vernonry, as she calls it."

"It is a little hard upon them to be called dependents; my old people live there. They have their own little income to live upon. Miss Vernon gives them their house, I believe, which is very kind, but not enough to justify the name of pensioners."

"That is our way here," said Edward laughing. "We are very ready to give, but we like to take the good of it. It is not respectful to call the place the Vernonry, but we do it. We are delighted to be kind; the more you will take from us, the better we will like you. We even—rather like you to be ungrateful. It satisfies our theory."

"Vernon, all that seems to me to be diabolical, you know, I wish you wouldn't. Miss Hester is a little of your way of thinking, I fear. She makes it amusing though. There are parties, it appears, where she stands all night in a corner, or looks at photographs."

"She says that, does she?" said Edward. His smile had not been a pleasant one, but now it disappeared from his face. "And I suppose she tells you that I never go near her? I have to look after the old ladies and take them to supper. I have the honour of standing in the position of master of the house."

"I don't know that she blames any one," said Ashton indifferently. "It is more fun than anger. Talk of want of air, Vernon; that poor child wants air if you please. She is as full of spirit and life as any one I ever saw. She would like to do something."

"Something! What kind of something? Go on the stage—or what?"

"I have never heard of the stage or anything of the kind. She wants work."

"Excitement!" Edward said, with an impatient gleam in his eyes.

"She is like you then," said Ashton, trying to laugh, but not with much cordiality, for he felt himself growing angry in spite of himself.

There was excitement enough now in Edward Vernon's face. It grew dark with passion and intolerance.

"A woman is altogether different," he said; then subduing himself with a change in his voice from rage to scorn, "she will soon have it in her power to change all that. Don't you know she is going to marry Harry Vernon?—an excellent match for her—money and little brains—whereas she has much brains and little money, the very thing in marriage," he concluded, with a harsh laugh.

"Is that so?" said Ashton.

He had been listening quite at his ease, turning his face towards his companion, and it was a satisfaction to Edward to see that the stranger's countenance clouded over. He was astonished, and Edward could not help hoping more than astonished—for being sore and bitter himself he liked to see another feel the sting.

"That's well," Roland said after a moment, "if she likes it. I should not have thought—but a week's acquaintance does not show you much of a character. I am glad to hear it," he said, after a pause, "if she likes it," which was but a dubious sort of satisfaction after all.

Edward looked at him again with an expression of gratified feeling. He was glad to have given his new friend a little friendly stab. It pleased him to see Roland wince. When one is very uneasy one's self, that is always a little consolation. He looked at him and enjoyed it, then turned away from the subject which had given him this momentary pleasure.

"Let us return to our muttons," he said. "Tell me what you think of these papers? I put them into my pocket to show you. Now that we are fairly out of sight"—then he turned back to glance along the still damp road, upon which there was not a single shadow but their own—"and nobody can spy upon us—for I distrust windows—we may think of business a little," the young man said.

Ashton looked at him as he took the papers with a glance as suspicious as his own. They had grown into a sort of sudden intimacy in a single night. Edward had been exactly in the state of mind to which Roland's revelation of chances and possibilities was as flame to tinder. To have his impatient desires and longings made practical was everything to him, and the prudence and business instinct left in him which made him hesitate to make the plunge by himself without skilled guidance, endowed the newcomer with an importance which nothing else could have given him. He was at home in those regions which were so entrancing and exciting, yet strange to Edward. These communications had brought them to something like confidential friendship, and yet they did not know each other, and in many things were mutually antipathetic, repelling, rather than attracting each other. This interview, though it was to seal the connection between them, made their mutual want of sympathy more apparent. Edward had showed the worst side of himself, and knew it. He felt even that his self-betrayal had been so great as to put him almost in his companion's power, while at the same time Ashton had impertinently interposed in the family affairs (a point upon which Edward was as susceptible as any one) by what he had permitted himself to say about Hester. Ashton, on the other hand, whose temper in a way was generous and easy, regarded the fortunate but ungrateful possessor of Catherine Vernon's sympathies with an indignant astonishment. To have been so taken up by such a woman, to have her affection, her confidence, her unbounded approbation and trust, and to so repay her! It was incredible, and the fellow was—— Should he fling up all his pretence at sympathy with this cub, and go off at once, rather abandoning the possible advantage than consenting to ally himself with such a being? This was the point at which they stood for a moment; but beside the pull of mutual interest how were they ever to explain the sudden breach, should they follow their mutual inclinations and make one? It would be necessary to say something, and what could be said? and then there lay before Edward a world of fabulous gain, of sudden wealth, of a hundred excitements to which Roland seemed to hold the key; and before Roland the consciousness that not only the advantage of having Edward, but a whole population of eager country people ready to put their money into his hands, and give him such power of immediate action as he had scarcely dreamt of, depended upon his self-restraint. Accordingly the sole evidence of their absolute distrust and dislike of each other, was this mutual look, exchanged just before they entered upon the closest relations of mutual aid.

It was a curious scene for such a beginning. The solitude of the country road was complete; there was no one to interrupt them. Although they were in the freedom of the open air, and subject to be overtaken by any passer-by, yet the Sunday stillness was so intense that they might have been in the most secret retirement on earth. Had they been seated together in Edward's room at home, a hundred disturbances were possible. Servants can never be shut out; if it is only to mend the fire they will appear in the middle of the most private conference. And Catherine herself, all unconscious that her presence was disagreeable, might have come to the door to summon them, or perhaps even to bring them, with her own kind hands, the cups of tea which in his heart Edward loathed as one of the signs of his slavery. They were the drink of bondage—those poor cups that never inebriate. He hated even the fragrance of them—the little steams ascending. Thank Heaven no one could bring him tea out upon the high road! The chill outer air, the faint scent of mossy damp and decay, the dim atmosphere without a sparkle in it, the absolute quiet, would have better suited confidences of a different description. But if business is not sentimental it is at least so urgent and engrossing, that it becomes indifferent to circumstances. The do-nothing calm of the Sunday closed curiously around the group; their rustling papers and eager countenances brought the strangest interruption of restless life into the almost dead and blank quiet. The season, the weather, the hour, the brown quiescent fields in which for the only moment of the year no mystery of growth was going on, but only a silent waiting for the seeds and the spring; this day of leisure when everything was at rest, all the surrounding circumstances united to throw into full relief the strange centre to the landscape—the two figures which brought a sharp interest of life into this still-breathing atmosphere, and waiting stagnation, and Sunday calm.

CHAPTER IV
ROLAND

Roland Ashton had been in little doubt as to his own motives when he came after so many years' indifference to "look up" his old grandparents, and take up late, yet not too late, the traditions of filial duty. These traditions, indeed, had no existence for this young man. His mother, the victim of a dissipated and hopeless spendthrift, had died when her children were young, and her father and mother had stood aloof from all but the earliest years of the handful of boys and girls she left behind. The children scrambled up somehow, and, as is not unusual among children, whom the squalor of a parent's vice has disgusted from their earliest consciousness, succeeded in doing well; the girls making much better marriages than could have been hoped for; the boys, flung into the world on their own account at a very early age, finding the means of maintaining themselves, and even pushing forward to a position as good as that which their father had lost. That father had happily died and gone out of all power to injure them, a number of years before, and it was only on a rare visit to the elder sister, who alone knew much about the family connections, that Roland had learned something of the state of affairs at Redborough.

Elinor was old enough to remember the time when the grandfather and grandmother had taken charge of the little weeping band of babies in their far-off helpless days, and she had kept up a certain correspondence with them, when, half ruined by that effort, they were saved by Catherine Vernon, the mysterious, wealthy cousin, of whose name everybody in the family had heard. Elinor remembered so many details when her memory was jogged, that it occurred to Roland that it would be a very good thing to go down to Redborough and pay his grandfather a visit. Catherine Vernon might turn out to be worth cultivating. She had stepped in to save old Captain Morgan and his wife from the consequences of their own liberality to their daughter's children. She had a little colony of pensioners about her, Elinor was informed. She was very rich, so rich that she did not know what to do with her money. There was a swarm of Vernons round her, eating her up.

"We are her nearest relations on her mother's side," Elinor had said. "I do not see why we should not have our chance too. Don't forget us, Roland, if you make any way; and you ought to do something; for you have the right way with women," his sister said, with some admiration and a little doubt. Her faith was that he was sure to succeed, her doubt whether his success would be of use to anybody but himself; but however it might turn out, it was always better that one of the Ashtons should benefit by Catherine Vernon's colossal fortune, than that it should all go into the hands of the other people.

Roland himself was well aware that he had the right way with women. This was not the result of art and calculation, but was pure nature. The young man was bent upon his own ends, without much consideration, in great matters, of other people. But in small matters he was very considerate, and had a delightful way of deferring to the comfort of those about him. And he had the power of looking interested, and even of feeling interested in everybody he addressed. And he had fine eyes! What more is needed to enable a young man to make his way with women? He was very popular; he might have married well had he chosen to take that step; indeed, the chief thing against him was, that he had wavered too long more than once, before he could make up his mind to hurt the feelings of a sensitive girl by not asking her to marry him. It was not, to be sure, his fault, if they thought that was his meaning. A prudent girl will never allow herself to think so until she is asked point-blank; and when you came to investigate each case, there really was nothing against Roland. He had made himself agreeable, but then, that was his way. He could not help making himself agreeable. The very tone of his voice changed when he spoke to any woman who pleased him, and he was very catholic in his tastes. Most women pleased him if they had good looks, or even the remains of good looks; or if they were clever; or even if they were *nice*; and he was pleasant to all, old and young. The quality was not without its dangers; but it had great advantages. He came to Redborough fully determined to make the conquest of Catherine Vernon, whom, save that she was rich and benevolent, he knew very little about. Very rich (according to Elinor), rather foolishly benevolent, old—a young man who has the right way with women could scarcely be indifferent to such a description. He determined to find an opportunity in the dull time of the year, when business was not too exacting, to pay some of the long over-due respect and gratitude which he owed to his grandfather. Captain Morgan professed to have cut himself clear of all his relationships, but it was true that twenty years before, he had spent everything he had, and deprived himself of every comfort, he and his wife, for the maintenance of his daughter's children. He had never got any return for this from the children, who knew very little about him. And it was full time that Roland should come with his power of making himself agreeable to pay the family debt—no harm if he did something for the family fortunes by the way.

And it has been seen that the young man fully proved, and at once, the justice of his sister's description of him. His grandmother, to be sure, was vanquished by his very name, by a resemblance which she found out in his mouth and eyelids to his mother, and by the old love which had never been extinguished, and could not be extinguished in her motherly old bosom. But Hester, by a mere chance encounter in the fire-light, without even seeing him, without knowing his name, had been moved to a degree of interest such as she was not conscious of having ever felt before. And Catherine Vernon had yielded at once, and without a struggle, to his influence. This was delightful enough, but after all it did not come to very much, for Roland found himself plunged into the midst of a society upon which he had not at all reckoned. The community at the Vernonry was simple; he was prepared for that, and understood it. But when he went to the Grange and made acquaintance with the closer circle there, the young men to whom Catherine had made over the bank and all its interests, and especially Edward, who was established as if he had been her son, in her house, a change came over Roland's plans and anticipations. He had a strong desire for his own advantage, and inclination to follow that wherever it might lead him; but he was not malignant in his selfishness. He had no wish to interfere, unless it proved to be absolutely necessary, with another man's career, or to injure his fellow-creatures in promoting his own interest. And it cannot be denied that he felt a shock of disappointment which, as he found when he reasoned with himself on the subject, was somewhat unreasonable. How could he expect the field to be clear for him, and the rich, childless woman of fortune left at his mercy? As if there were not crowds of other people in the world who had a quick eye for their own advantage, and clear sight to see who was likely to serve it! But these discoveries put him out. They made his mission purposeless. They reduced it to the mere visit to his grandfather, which he had called it, but which he by no means intended it solely to be.

After this first shock of disappointment, however, Roland began to find himself at once amused and interested by the new community, into the midst of which he had dropped. The inmates of the Vernonry were all simple enough. To be very poor and obliged to accept favours from a rich relative, yet never to be able to escape the sense of humiliation, and a grudge against those who are better off—that is indeed too general: and it is even a conventional necessity of the imagination, that there should be bickerings and private little spites among neighbours so closely thrown together. Ashton did not see much of the Miss Vernon-Ridgways, who had refused to know him at Catherine's house, nor of their kindred spirit Mr. Mildmay Vernon; but he could imagine them, and did so easily. Nor was the gentle little widow, who was now on one side now on the other, according as the last speaker moved her, or the young heroine her daughter, difficult to realise. But Catherine, and the closer group of her relations, puzzled him more. That she should gauge them all so exactly, yet go on with them, pouring kindness upon their ungrateful heads with a sort of amusement at their ingratitude, almost a malicious pleasure in it, surprised him less than that among all who surrounded her there was no one who gave to her a real and faithful devotion. And her faith in Edward, whose impatience of her bonds was the greatest of all, seemed to Roland in his spectatorship so pitiful, that he could scarcely help crying out against it to earth and heaven. He was sorry for her all the more that she was so little sorry for herself, and it seemed to him that of all her surroundings he was the only one who was sorry for Catherine. Even his old people as he called them, did not fathom that curse of her loneliness. They thought with everybody else that Edward was a true son to her, studying her wishes, and thinking of nothing so much as how to please her. It appalled him when he thought of the snarl on Edward's lips, the profound discontent in his soul. It would be cruel above all things to warn her—she who felt herself so clear-sighted—of the deception she was the victim of; and yet what could it come to but unhappiness? Roland felt himself overpowered and almost overawed by this combination. Nobody but he, it seemed, had divined it. He had walked back with Edward to the Grange after their long talk and consultation, and had taken off his hat with a smile of kindness to the indistinct figure still seated in the window, which Edward recognised with a secret grimace. To see her seated there looking out for their return, was a pleasure to the more genial spirit. It would have pleased him to feel that there was some one who would look out for his coming, who would watch him like this, with tenderness as he went away. But then he had no experience of the kind in his own person, and Edward perhaps had too much of it. While the one went indoors with a bitter sense that he could go nowhere without being watched, the other turned away with a pleasant look back, waving his hand to Catherine Vernon in the window. She was not likely to adopt him, but she was kind to him, a pleasant, handsome old woman, and a most creditable relative. He was glad he had come if it were for that and no more. There were other reasons too why Roland should be glad he had come. He had found a new client, nay, a group of new clients, by whose means he could extend his business and his prospects—solid people with real money to risk, not men of straw. Though he was full of aspirations they were all of a practical kind. He meant to make his fortune; he meant to do the very best for his customers who trusted him as well as for himself, and his spirits rose when he thought what a power of extensive and successful operation would be given him by the money of all these new people who were so eager to face the risks of speculation. They should not suffer by it; their confidence in him should be repaid, and not only his, but their fortunes would be made.

The certainty of this went to his head a little, like wine. It had been well for him to come. It had been the most important step he had ever taken in his life. It was not what he had hoped for, and yet it was the thing above all others that he wanted, a new start for him in the world, and probably the turning-point of his life. Other matters were small in comparison with this, and approbation or disappointment has little to do with a new customer in any branch of business. As for other interests he might have taken up on the way, the importance of them was nothing. Hester was a pretty girl, and it was natural to him to have an occupation of that sort in hand; but to suppose that he was sufficiently interested to allow any thought of her to beguile him from matters so much more serious, would have been vain indeed. He felt just such a momentary touch of pique in hearing that she was going to be married, as a woman-beauty does when she hears of any conquests but her own. If she had seen him (Roland) first, she would not have been, he felt, so easily won; but he laughed at himself for the thought, as perhaps the woman-beauty would scarcely have been moved to do.

CHAPTER V
WARNING

"I think, if you will let me, I will send down Emma for a little fresh air and to make your acquaintance, grandmother. She is rather of the butterfly order of girls, but there is no harm in her. And as it is likely that I shall have a good deal to do with the Vernons— —"

"What do you want with the Vernons? Why should you have a good deal to do with them?" asked Captain Morgan, hastily, and it must be added rather testily, for the old man's usually placid humour had been disturbed of late.

"In the most legitimate way," said Ashton. "You can't wish me, now that I am just launched in business, to shut my eyes to my own advantage. It will be for their advantage too. They are going to be customers of mine. When you have a man's money to invest you have a good deal to do with him. I shall have to come and go in all likelihood often."

"Your customers—and their money to invest—what do mean by that? I hope you haven't taken advantage of my relationship with Catherine Vernon to draw in those boys of hers— —"

"Grandfather," said Roland, with an *air digne* which it was impossible not to respect, "if you think a little you will see how injurious your words are. I cannot for a moment suppose you mean them. Catherine Vernon's boys, as you call them, are nearly as old, and I suppose as capable of judging what is for their advantage, as I am. If they choose to entrust me with their business, is there any reason why I should refuse it? I am glad to get everything I can."

"Yes, sir, there is a reason," said Captain Morgan. "I know what speculation is. I know what happens when a hot-headed young fellow gets a little bit of success, and the gambling fever gets into his veins. Edward Vernon is just the sort of fellow to fall a victim. He is a morose, ill-tempered, bilious being— —"

"Stop," said Roland; "have a little consideration, sir. There is no question of any victim."

"You are just a monomaniac, Rowley, my old man," said Mrs. Morgan.

"I know everything you can say," said the old captain. "All that jargon about watching the market, and keeping a cool head, and running no unnecessary risks—I know it all. You think you can turn over your money, as you call it, always to your advantage, and keep risk at arm's length."

"I do not say so much as that; but risk may be reduced to a minimum, and profit be the rule, when one gives one's mind to it—which it is my business to do."

"Oh, I know everything you can say," said the old man. "Give your mind to it! Give your mind to an honest trade, that's my advice to you. What is it at the best but making money out of the follies of your fellow-creatures? They take a panic and you buy from them, to their certain loss, and then they take a freak of enthusiasm and you sell to them, to their certain loss. Somebody must always lose in order that you should gain. It is a devilish trade—I said so when I heard you had gone into it; but for God's sake, Roland Ashton, keep that for the outside world, and don't bring ruin and misery here."

"What can I say?" said the young man. He rose up from the table where he had been taking his last meal with the old people. He kept his temper beautifully, Mrs. Morgan thought, with great pride in him. He grew pale and a little excited, as was natural, but never forgot his respect for his grandfather, who, besides that venerable relationship, was an old man. "What can I say? To tell you that I consider my profession an honourable one would be superfluous, for you can't imagine I should have taken it up had I thought otherwise."

"Rowley, my old man," said Mrs. Morgan, "you are just as hot-headed as when you were a boy. But, Roland, you must remember that we have suffered from it; and everybody says when you begin to gamble in business, it is worse than any other kind of gambling."

"When you begin; but there is no need ever to begin, that I can see."

"And then, my dear—I am not taking up your grandfather's view, but just telling you what he means—then, my dear, Catherine Vernon has been very kind to him and me. She is fond of us, I really believe. She trusts us, which to her great hurt, poor thing, she does to few——"

"Catherine Vernon is a noble character. She has a fine nature. She has a scorn of meanness and everything that is little——"

The old lady shook her head, "That is true," she said; "but it is her misfortune, poor thing, that she gets her amusement out of all that, and she believes in few. You must not, Roland," she said, laying her hand upon his arm, "you must not, my dear lad—Oh, listen to what my old man says! You must not be the means of leading into imprudence or danger any one she is fond of—she that has been so kind to him and to me!"

The old hand was heavy on his arm, bending him down towards her with an imperative clasp, and this sudden appeal was so unexpected from the placid old woman, who seemed to have outgrown all impassioned feeling and lived only to soothe and reconcile opposing influences, that both the young man and the old were impressed by it. Roland Ashton stooped, and kissed his grandmother's forehead. He had a great power in him of response to every call of emotion.

"Dear old mother," he said, "if I were a villain and meant harm, I don't see how I could carry on with it after that. But I want you to believe that I am not a villain," he said, with a half-laugh of feeling.

Old Captain Morgan was so touched by the scene that in the weakness of old age and the unexpectedness of this interposition the tears stood in his eyes.

"When you do put your shoulder to the wheel, Mary," he said, with a half-laugh too, and holding out a hand to Roland, with whom for the first time he found himself in perfect sympathy, "you do it like a hero. I'll add nothing to what she has said, my boy. Even at the risk of losing a profit, or failing in a stroke of business, respect the house that has sheltered your family. That's what we both say."

"And I have answered, sir," said Roland, "that even if I were bent on mischief I could not persist after such an appeal—and I am not bent on mischief," he added, this time with a smile; and so fell into easy conversation about his sister, and the good it would do her to pay the old people a visit. "I am out all day, and she is left to herself. It is dull for her in a little house at Kilburn, all alone—though she says she likes it," he went on, glad, as indeed they all were, to get down to a milder level of conversation.

The old captain had not taken kindly to the idea of having Emma; but after the moment of sympathetic emotion which they had all passed through, there was no rejecting so very reasonable a petition. And on the whole, looking back upon it, now that the young man's portmanteau stood packed in the hall, and he himself was on the eve of departure, even the captain could not deny that there had been on the whole more pleasure in Roland's visit than he had at all expected. However he might modify the account of his own sensations, it had certainly been agreeable to meet a young fellow of his own blood, his descendant, a man among the many women with whom he was surrounded, and one who, even when they disagreed, could support his opinions, and was at least intelligent, whatever else. He had received him with unfeigned reluctance, almost forgetting who his mother was in bitter and strong realisation that he was his father's son and bore his father's name. But personal encounter had so softened everything, that though Roland actually resembled his objectionable father, the captain parted from him with regret. And, after all, why should not Emma come? She was a girl, which in itself softened everything (notwithstanding that the captain had recognised as a distinct element in Roland's favour that he was a man, and so a most desirable interruption to the flood of womankind—but nobody is bound to be consistent in these matters). It was good of her brother, as soon as he was afloat in the world, to take upon himself the responsibility of providing for Emma, and on the whole the captain, always ready to be kind, saw no reason for refusing to be kind to this lonely girl because she was of his own flesh and blood. He drew much closer to his grandson during these last few hours than he had done yet. He went out with him to make his adieux to Mrs. John and her daughter. And Hester came forward to give them her hand with that little enlargement about the eyes, which was a sure sign of some emotion in her mind. She had seen a great deal of Roland, and his going away gave her a pang which she scarcely explained to herself. It was so much life subtracted from the scanty circle. She too, like Edward, felt that she wanted air, and the departure of one who had brought so much that was new into her restricted existence was a loss—that was all. She had assured herself so half-a-dozen times this morning—therefore no doubt it was true. As for Roland, it was not in him to part from such a girl without an attempt at least to intensify this effect. He drew her towards the window, apart from the others, to watch, as he said, for the coming of the slow old fly from Redborough which was to convey him away.

"My sister is coming," he said, "and I hope you will be friends. I will instruct her to bring in my name on every possible occasion, that you may not altogether forget me."

"There is no likelihood that we shall forget you; we see so few people here."

"And you call that a consolatory reason! I shall see thousands of people, but I shall not forget *you*." It was Roland's way to use no name. He said *you* as if there was nobody but yourself who owned that pronoun, with an inference that in thinking of the woman before him, whoever she might be, he, in his heart, identified her from all women.

Hester was embarrassed by his eyes and his tone, but not displeased. He had pleased her from the first. There is a soft and genial interest excited in the breasts of women by such a man, at which everybody smiles and which few acknowledge, yet which is not the less dangerous for that. It rouses a prepossession in his favour, whatever may come of it afterwards; and he had done his best to fill up all his spare moments, when he was not doing something else, in Hester's company. It would be vain to say that this homage had not been sweet, and it had been entertaining, which is so great a matter. It had opened out a new world to her, and expanded all her horizon. With his going all these new outlets into life would be closed again. She felt a certain terror of the place without Roland. He had imported into the air an excitement, an expectation. The prospect of seeing him was a prospect full of novelty and interest, and even when he did not come, there had always been that expectation to brighten the dimness. Now there could be no expectation, not even a disappointment; and Hester's eyes were large, and had a clearness of emotion in them. She might have cried—indeed, it seemed very likely that she had cried at the thought of his going away, and would cry again.

"Though I don't know," he added, leaning against the recess of the window, and so shutting her in where she stood looking out, "why I should leave so many thoughts here, for I don't suppose they will do me any good. They tell me that your mind will be too fully, and, alas, too pleasantly occupied. Yes, I say alas! and alas again! I am not glad you will be so pleasantly occupied. I had rather you were dull a little, that you might have time now and then to remember me."

"You are talking a great deal of nonsense, Mr. Ashton—but that is your way. And how am I to be so pleasantly occupied? I am glad to hear it, but I certainly did not know. What is going to happen?"

"Is this hypocrisy, or is it kindness to spare me? Or is it——? They tell me that I ought to—congratulate you," said Roland with a sigh.

"Congratulate me? On what? I suppose," said Hester, growing red, "there is only one thing upon which girls are congratulated: and that does not exist in my case."

"May I believe you?" he said, putting his hands together with a supplicating gesture, "may I put faith in you? But it seemed on such good authority. Your cousin Edward——"

"Did Edward tell you so?" Hester grew so red that the flush scorched her. She was angry and mortified and excited. Her interest changed, in a moment, from the faint interest which she had felt in the handsome young deceiver before her, to a feeling more strong and deeply rooted, half made out of repulsion, half bitter, half injured, yet more powerful in attraction than any other sentiment of her mind. Roland was ill-pleased that he was superseded by this other feeling. It was a sensation quite unusual to him, and he did not like it. "He had no right to say so," said Hester; "he knew it was not true."

"All is fair in love and war," said Roland; "perhaps he wished it to be—not true."

"I do not know what he wishes, and I do not care!" Hester cried, after a pause, with a passion which did not carry out her words. "He has never been a friend to me," she said hastily. "He might have helped me, he might have been kind—not that I want his help or any one's," cried the girl, her passion growing as she went on. Then she came to a dead stop, and gave Roland a rapid look, to see how much he had divined of her real feelings. "But he need not have said what was not true," she added in a subdued tone.

"I forgive him," said Roland, "because it is not true. If it had been true it would not have been so easy to forgive. I am coming back again, and I should have seen you—changed. It was too much. Now I can look forward with unmingled pleasure. It is one's first duty, don't you think, to minister to the pleasure of one's grandparents? they are old; one ought to come often, as often as duty will permit."

Hester looked up to him with a little surprise, the transition was so sudden; and, to tell the truth, the tumult in her own mind was not so entirely subdued that she could bestow her full attention upon Roland's *double entendre*.

He laughed. "One would think, by your look, that you did not share my fine sense of duty," he said; "but you must not frown upon it. I am coming soon, very soon, again. A fortnight ago the place was only a name to me; but now it is a name that I shall remember for ever," he added with fervour.

Hester looked at him this time with a smile upon her mouth. She had recovered herself and come back to the diversion of his presence, the amusement and novelty he had brought. A half sense of the exaggeration and sentimental nonsense of his speech was in her smile; and he was more or less conscious of it too. When their eyes met they both laughed; and yet she was not displeased, nor he untouched by some reality of feeling. The exaggeration was humorous, and the sentiment not altogether untrue.

"Do you say that always when you leave a place?" Hester said.

"Very often," he acknowledged; and they both laughed again, which, to her at least, was very welcome, as she had been doubly on the verge of tears—for anger and for regret. "But seldom as I do now," he added, "you may believe me. The old people are better and kinder than I had dreamt of; it does one good to be near them; and then I have helped myself on in the world by this visit, but that you will not care for. And then——"

Here Roland broke off abruptly, and gazed, as his fashion was, as feeling the impotence of words to convey all that the heart would say.

It was very shortly after this that the white horse which drew the old fly from Redborough—the horse which was supposed to have been chosen for this quality, that it could be seen a long way off to console the souls of those who felt it could never arrive in time—was seen upon the road, and the last moment had visibly come. Not the less for the commotion and tumult or other feelings through which her heart had gone, did Hester acknowledge the emotions which belonged to this leave-taking. The depth and sadness of Roland's eyes—those expressive eyes which said so many things, the pathos of his mouth, the lingering clasp in which he held her hand, all affected her. There was a magic about him which the girl did not resist, though she was conscious of the other side of it, the faint mixture of the fictitious which did not impair its charm. She stood and watched him from the low window of the parlour which looked that way, while the fly was being laden, with a blank countenance. She felt the corners of her mouth droop, her eyes widen, her face grow longer. It was as if all the novelty, the variety, the pleasure of life were going away. It was a dull afternoon, which was at once congenial as suiting the circumstances and oppressive as enhancing the gloom. She watched the portmanteau put in as if she had been watching a funeral. When Roland stepped in after his grandfather, who in the softness of the moment had offered, to the great surprise of everybody, to accompany him to the station, Hester still looked on with melancholy gravity. She was almost on a level with them where she stood looking out; her mother all smiles, kissing her hand beside her. "I wish you would show a little interest, Hester," Mrs. John said. "You might at least wave your hand. If it were only for the old captain's sake whom you always profess to be so fond of." Roland at this moment leant out of the window of the fly and took off his hat to her for the last time. Mrs. John thought it was barbarous to take no notice. She redoubled her own friendly salutations; but Hester stood like a statue, forcing a faint ghost of a smile, but not moving a finger. She stood thus watching them long after they had driven away, till they had almost disappeared in the smoke of Redborough. She saw the fly stop at the Grange and Miss Catherine come out to the door to take leave of him: and then the slow vehicle disappeared altogether. The sky seemed to lean down almost touching the ground; the stagnant afternoon air had not a breath to move it. Hester said to herself that nothing more would happen now. She knew the afternoon atmosphere, the approach of tea, the scent of it in the air, the less ethereal bread-and-butter, and then the long dull evening. It seemed endless to look forward, as if it never would be night. And Mrs. John, as soon as the fly was out of sight, had drawn her chair towards the fire and begun to talk. "I am sure I am very sorry he has gone," Mrs. John said. "I did not think I should have liked him at first, but I declare I like him very much now. How long is it since he came, Hester? Only a fortnight! I should have said three weeks at least. I think it was quite unnatural of the captain to talk of him as he did, for I am sure he is a very nice young man. Where are you going? not I hope for one of your long walks: for the night closes in very early now, and it will soon be time for tea."

"Don't you think, mamma," said Hester, somewhat hypocritically, "that it would be kind to go in and keep Mrs. Morgan company a little, as she will be quite alone?"

"That is always your way as soon as I show any inclination for a little talk," said her mother provoked, not without reason. Then she softened, being at heart the most good-natured of women. "Perhaps you are right," she said, "the old lady will be lonely. Give her my love, and say I should have come to see her myself, but that—" Mrs. John paused for a reason, "but that I am afraid for my neuralgia," she added triumphantly. "You know how bad it was the other day."

Thus sanctioned Hester threw her grey "cloud" round her, and ran round to console Mrs. Morgan, while her mother arranged herself comfortably with a footstool, a book upon the table beside her, and her knitting, but with a furtive inclination towards an afternoon nap, which the greyness of the day, the early failing light in the dark wainscoted parlour, and the absence of all movement about her, naturally inclined her to. Mrs. John was at the age when we are very much ashamed of the afternoon nap, and she was well provided with semblances of occupation in case any one should come. But Mrs. Morgan was far beyond any such simple deceit. Eighty has vast advantages in this way. When she felt disposed to doze a little she was quite pleased, almost proud of the achievement. She had indeed a book on the table with her spectacles carefully folded into it, but she did not require any occupation.

"I had a kind of feeling that you would come, my pet," she said as Hester appeared. "When I want you very much I think some kind little angel must go and tap you on the shoulder, for you always come."

"The captain would say it is a brain-wave," said Hester.

"The captain says a great deal of nonsense, my dear," said the old lady with a smile, "but think of him going with Roland to the station! He has been vanquished, quite vanquished—which is a great pleasure to me. And Emma is coming. I hope she will not wear out the good impression——"

"Is she not so—nice?" Hester asked.

The old lady looked her favourite intently in the face. She saw the too great clearness of Hester's eyes, and that her mouth was not smiling, but drawn downward; and a vague dread filled her mind. She was full of love and charity, but she was full of insight too; and though she loved Roland, she did not think it would be to the advantage of Hester to love him.

"Roland is very nice," she said. "Poor boy, perhaps that is his temptation. It is his nature to please whomsoever he comes across. It is a beautiful kind of nature; but I am not sure that it is not very dangerous both for himself—and others."

It was fortunate that Hester did not divine what her friend meant.

"Dangerous—to please?" she said, with a little curiosity. She liked Roland so much, that even from the lips of those who had more right to him than she had, she did not like to hear blame.

"To wish to please—everybody," said the old lady. "My poor lad! that is his temptation. Your grandfather, if he were here—my dear, I beg your pardon. I have got into the way of saying it: as if my old man was your grandfather too."

"I like it," Hester said, with the only gleam of her usual frank and radiant smile which Mrs. Morgan had yet seen. But this made the old lady only more afraid.

"There is nobody he could be more fatherly to," she said. "What I meant was that if he were here, he would have something ready out of a book, as you and he are always going on with your poetries; but I never was a poetry woman, as you know. Life is all my learning. And I have seen people that have had plenty of heart, Hester, if they had given it fair play—but frittered it away on one and another, trying to give a piece to each, making each believe that she (for it is mostly upon women that the spell works) was the one above all others. But you are so young, my darling; you will not know what I mean."

A faint, uneasy colour, came on Hester's face.

"I think I know what you mean," she said. "I understand how you should think so of Mr. Ashton. You don't see so well as you did, dear Mrs. Morgan, when you have not got your spectacles on. If you did, you would see that when he talks like *that*, he is ready to laugh all the time."

"Is that so, my love? Then I am very glad to hear you say so," cried the old lady. But she knew very well that her supposed want of sight was a delusion, and that Hester knew it was only for reading that she ever used her spectacles. She felt, however, all the more that her warning had been taken, and that it was unnecessary to proceed further. "You are young and sweet," she said, "my dear: but the best thing still is that you have sense. Oh, what it is to have sense! it is the best blessing in life."

Hester made no reply to this praise. Her heart was beating more quickly than usual. What she had said was quite true: but all the time, though he had been ready to laugh, and though she had been ready to laugh, she was aware that there was something more. The tone of banter had not been all. The sense of something humorous, under those high-flown phrases, had not exhausted them. She was intended to laugh, indeed, if they did not secure another sentiment; but the first aim, and perhaps the last aim, of the insidious Roland, had been to secure this other sentiment. Hester did not enter into these distinctions, but she felt them; and when she thus put forward Mrs. Morgan's failing sight, it was with a natural casuistry which she knew would be partially seen through, and yet would have its effect. This made her feel that there was no reply to be made to the praise of her "sense," which the old lady had given. Was it her cunning that the old lady meant to praise? There was a little silence, and the subject of Roland was put aside, not perhaps quite to the satisfaction of either; but there was nothing more that could be said.

And presently the old captain came back, groaning a little over his long walk.

"Why do you never remind me," he said, "what an old fool I am? To drive in that jingling affair, and to walk back—two miles if it is a yard—well, then, a mile and a half. My dear, what was half a mile when you and I were young is two miles now, and not an inch less; but I have seen him off the premises. And now, Hester, we shall have our talks again, and our walks again, without any interruption——"

"Do not speak so fast, Rowley. There is Emma coming; and Hester will like a girl to talk with, and to walk with, better than an old fellow like you."

"That old woman insults me," said the captain. "She thinks I am as old as she is—but Hester, you and I know better. You are looking anxious, my child. Do you think we are a frivolous old pair talking as we ought not—two old fools upon the brink of the grave?"

"Captain Morgan! I, to have such a thought! And what should I do without you?" cried Hester, in quick alarm. This brought the big tears to her eyes, and perhaps she was glad, for various causes, to have a perfectly honest and comprehensible cause in the midst of her agitation, for those tears.

"This was brought to my mind very clearly to-day," said the old captain. "When I saw that young fellow go off, a man in full career of his life, and thought of his parents swept away, the mother whom you know I loved, Mary, as dearly as a man ever loves his child, and the father whom I hated, both so much younger than we are, and both gone for years; and here are we still living, as if we had been forgotten somehow. We just go on in our usual, from day to day, and it seems quite natural; but when you think of all of them—gone—and we two still here——"

"We are not forgotten," said the old lady, in her easy chair, smiling upon him, folding those old hands which were now laid up from labour, hands that had worked hard in their day. "We have some purpose to serve yet, or we would not be here."

"I suppose so—I suppose so," said the old man, with a sigh; and then he struck his stick upon the floor, and cried out, "but not, God forbid it, as the instruments of evil to the house that has sheltered us, Mary! My heart misgives me. I would like at least, before anything comes of it, that we should be out of the way, you and I."

"You were always a man of little faith," his wife said. "Why should you go out of your way to meet the evil, that by God's good grace will never come? It will never come; we have not been preserved for that. You would as soon teach me Job's lesson as to believe that, my old man."

"What was Job's lesson? It was, 'Though He slay me, yet will I trust in Him,'" Captain Morgan said.

"Oh, my Rowley!" cried the old lady, "I was wrong to say you were of little faith! It is you that are the faithful one, and not me. I am just nothing beside you, as I have always been."

The old captain took his wife's old hands in his, and gave her a kiss upon her faded cheek, and they smiled upon each other, the two who had been one for nearly sixty years. Meanwhile, Hester sitting by, looked on with large eyes of wonder and almost affright. She did not know what it meant. She could not divine what it could be that made them differ, yet made them agree. What harm could they do to the house that sheltered them, two old, good, peaceful people, who were kind to everybody? She gazed at them with her wondering young eyes, and did what she could to fathom the mystery: then retired from it, thinking it perhaps some little fad of the old people, which she had no knowledge of, nor means of understanding. The best people, Hester thought, when they grew old take strange notions into their heads, and trouble themselves about nothing; and of course they missed Roland. She broke in upon them in that moment of feeling, as soon as she dared speak for wonder, making an effort to amuse them, and bring them back to their usual ways; and that effort was not in vain.

CHAPTER VI
DANCING TEAS

It was shortly after the departure of Roland that a new era dawned for Hester in social life. Mrs. Algernon Merridew had felt from the moment of her return from Abroad that there was a work for her to do in Redborough. It was not the same as in her maiden days, when she had been at the head of Harry's household, wonderfully enfranchised indeed, but still somewhat under the awe of Aunt Catherine. But now she was altogether independent, and nobody had any right to make suggestions as to who she should invite or how she should entertain, to a married lady, with an admiring husband, not to speak of brother—and sisters-in-law, eagerly anticipating social elevation by her means, at her back. Ellen was not ill-natured. She was very willing to promote the happiness and prosperity of others, so long as she could do so without any diminution of her own—a negative goodness which the world at large is very well pleased to acknowledge as satisfactory. And it is not at all probable that the representations of Harry, or the good-humoured suggestions of Algernon inspired by Harry, to the effect that it would be sublimely good of her to take up and brighten the life of Hester, would have come to very much, had it not at the same time occurred to Ellen that Hester was the best assistant she could have on her own side of the house, in the indispensable work of making her Thursdays "go." Rather than that they should not "go," she would have embraced her worst enemy, had she possessed one; and she did not care to rely upon the Merridew girls, feeling as she did that she had condescended in entering their family, and that they must never be allowed to forget that they owed everything to her, and she nothing to them. But at the same time she required a feminine auxiliary, a somebody to be her right hand, and help to make everything "go." The result of her cogitations on this subject was that she set out for the Vernonry one afternoon in the little victoria, which Algernon, rather tremulous about the cost, had set up for her, and which, with the smart coachman who for the moment condescended to be gardener too, and the boy on the box who was of quite a fashionable size, looked a very imposing little equipage. Ellen lay back in her little carriage enveloped in her new sealskin, with a little hat of the same upon her head, and a muff also of the same, and her light hair looking all the brighter against that dark background, with bracelets enough to make a jingle wherever she went, and which she had to push up upon her arm from time to time, and a violet scent about herself and all her garments, at least the scent which is called violet at Piesse and Lubin's, which served her purpose. When she drove up in this state, it may be supposed what a flutter she made in the afternoon atmosphere. The inmates of the Vernonry rushed to their windows.

"It is that little doll Ellen, come to show off more of her finery," said one sister.

"I wonder why she comes here, when you set her down so, Matilda," said the other.

They kept behind the curtains, one over the other's shoulder, that she might not see how curious they were. But when Ellen floated in at the verandah door, and was evidently gone to see Mrs. John, their astonishment was boundless. They shrugged their shoulders and interchanged glances with Mr. Mildmay Vernon, who, with his newspaper in his hand, had appeared at his window.

"Did he think she was going to see *him*?" Miss Matilda said, even while addressing these satires in pantomime to him. "What interest can he take in Ellen? It is just prying and curiosity, and nothing more."

The gentleman's comments were not more friendly. He chuckled as he saw where Ellen was going.

"The old cats will think it a visit to them, and they will be disappointed," he said to himself, all the same shrugging his shoulders back again to Miss Matilda. They kept on the watch all the time the visit lasted, and it was a long one. The sisters discussed the victoria, the horse, the little footman, the great fur rug which Ellen threw off as she jumped lightly out of the carriage. It was somewhat hard indeed that a little minx like Ellen should have all these things, and her seniors, her betters, who would have enjoyed them so much, none of them. But so it always is in this unjust world.

On the other side of the partition from where the sisters were sitting, Ellen's appearance had caused an almost equal sensation. She was not looked for, and the proposal she made was a very startling one.

"I am going to begin my *Thés Dansantes*, and I want you to help me," she said abruptly. "I want you to be my right hand; just like my sister. You know I can't do everything myself. Mrs. John, you shall come too, I never intended to leave you out; but I want Hester to help me, for she is the only one that can help me. She is really my cousin. Clara and Connie are only my sisters-in-law, and I don't care to have them about me in that position. It would be nice for me, and it would be giving Hester the best of chances. Now, Mrs. John, I am sure you will see it in that light. What could be better for a girl? All that she will meet will be the best sort of people: and she would have her chance."

"I don't know what you mean by having my chance—and I don't want any chance," said Hester, in a flush of shame and indignation; but Ellen put her down with a wave of her gloved hand and arm, all tinkling with bangles.

"Of course you don't know anything about it," she said, "an unmarried girl! We don't want you to know. Your mother and I will talk about that; but you can understand that a nice dance in a nice house like ours will be something pleasant. And you would be there not just like a visitor, but like one of the family, and get a good deal of attention, and as many partners as ever you liked."

"Of course, Ellen, of course," cried Mrs. John. "I am sure *I* understand you. It would be very nice for Hester. At her age every girl likes a little gaiety, and in my position I have never been able to give it to her. It was very different when my husband was alive, when we were in the White House. I am sure I have never grudged it to you, but it made a great difference. I was not brought up to this sort of thing. I had my balls, and my parties, as many as could be wished, when I was Hester's age. If her poor papa had lived, and we had stayed in the White House, she would have held a very different position. It gives me a little prick, you will understand, to think of Hester wanting anybody to be kind to her; but still, as it is so, and as you are her relation, I never could object. You will find no objection from me."

"No, I should think not," cried Ellen, throwing back her warm coat. It was at the time when sealskins were rare, when they were just "coming in," and Mrs. John looked at it with admiration. She did not ask, as the Miss Vernon-Ridgways did, why this little minx should have everything; but she remembered with a little regret the days when she too had everything that a young woman could desire, and wondered, with a little flutter at her heart, whether when Hester married she would have a sealskin and a victoria, and all the other crowns of happiness. She looked with something of a pathetic look at her daughter. Ah! if she could but see Hester as Ellen was!

Meanwhile Hester was elevating her young head as was natural, in special scorn of the "chance" which her cousin meant to secure for her, and in defiance altogether of the scheme, which nevertheless (for she was but human and nineteen, and the prospect of a dance every week took away her breath) moved her in spite of herself.

"When I was a child," Hester said, "when you first came to see us, Cousin Ellen, you said you must see a great deal of me, that I must go to your house, that you and Harry would take me out, that I should have a share in your pleasures. Perhaps my mother and you don't remember—but

I do. How I used to look out for you every morning; how I used to watch at the window, thinking they will surely come or send, or take some notice to-day. I was very young, you know, and believed everything, and wished so much to drive about and to go to parties. But you never came."

"To think she should remember all that!" cried Ellen, a little abashed. "Of course I didn't. Why, you were only a child. One said so to please you; but how can you suppose one meant anything? What could I have done with you then—a little thing among lots of people? Why, you wouldn't have been allowed to come! It would have been bad for you. You would have heard things you oughtn't to hear. You wouldn't have let her come, would you, Mrs. John?"

"Certainly not, my dear," said Mrs. John, promptly. To tell the truth, it was she who had complained the most though it was Hester who had been most indignant. She forgot this, however, in the new interest of the moment. "It would never have done," she said, with all sincerity. "Your cousin, of course, only spoke to please you, Hester. I never could have permitted you, a little thing at your lessons, to plunge into pleasure at that age."

"Then why—" cried Hester, open-mouthed; but when she had got so far she paused. What was the use of saying any more? She looked at them both with her large brown eyes, full of light and wonder, and a little indignation and a little scorn, then stopped and laughed, and changed the subject. "When I go to Cousin Catherine's," she said, "which I never do when I can help it, we stand in a corner all the evening, my mother and I. We are thankful when any one speaks to us—the curate's daughters and the Miss Reynoldses and we—— There is never anybody to take us in to supper. All the Redborough people sweep past while mamma stands waiting; and then perhaps some gentleman who has been down once before takes pity, and says, 'Haven't you been down to supper, Mrs. Vernon? Dear me! then let me take you.' You will please to remember that my mother is Mrs. Vernon, Ellen, and not Mrs. John."

"I only say it for—short," said Ellen, apologetically; "and how can I help what happens at Aunt Catherine's? I don't go in for her ways. I don't mean to do as she does. Why do you talk of Aunt Catherine to me?"

"It is only to let you see that I will not be treated so," the girl said with indignation. "If you think I will go to your house like that, just because you are a relation, I won't, Ellen; and you had better understand this before we begin."

"What a spitfire it is!" said Ellen, raising her hand with a toss of all her bracelets to brush Hester's downy cheek with a playful touch. "To think she should put all these things down in her book against us! I should never remember if it were me. I should be furious for the moment, and then I should forget all about it. Now, Hester, you look here. I am not asking you for your own pleasure, you silly; I am asking you to help *me*. Don't you see that makes all the difference? You are no good to Aunt Catherine. She doesn't need you. She asks you only for civility. But it stands to reason, you know, that I can't look after all the people myself if I am to have any of the fun. I must have some one to help me. Of course you will have every attention paid you; for, don't you see, you are wanted. I can't get on without you. Oh, *of course*, that makes all the difference! I am sure your mamma understands very well, even if you are too young and too silly to understand!"

"Yes, Hester, your cousin is quite right," said Mrs. John, eagerly. The poor lady was so anxious to secure her child's assent to what she felt would be so manifestly for her advantage that she was ready to back up everything that Ellen said. A spark of animation and new life had lighted up in Mrs. John's eyes. It was not a very elevated kind of hope perhaps, yet no hope that is centred in the successes of another is altogether ignoble. She wanted to see her child happy; she wanted Hester to have her chance, as Ellen said. That she should be seen and admired and made much of, was, Mrs. John felt, the first object in her life. It would not be without some cost to herself, but she did not shrink from the idea of the lonely evenings she would have to spend, or the separation that might ensue. Her mind, which was not a great mind, jumped forward into an instant calculation of how the evening dresses could be got, at what sacrifice of ease or comfort. She did not shrink from this, whatever it might be. Neither did she let any visionary pride stand in her way as Hester did. She was ready to forgive, to forget, to condone all offences—and in the long discussion and argument that followed, Mrs. John was almost more eloquent than Ellen on the mutual advantages of the contract. She saw them all the instant they were set before her. She was quite tremulous with interest and expectation. She ran over with approval and beaming admiration as Ellen unfolded her plans. "Oh, yes, I can quite understand; you want to strike out something original," cried Mrs. John. "You must not think I agree with Hester about Catherine's parties. I think Catherine's parties are very nice; and relations, you know, must expect to give way to strangers, especially when there are not enough of gentlemen; but it will be much pleasanter for you to strike out something original. I should have liked it when I was in your circumstances, but I don't think I had the energy. And I am sure if Hester can be of any use—— Oh, my darling! of course you will like it very much. You always are ready to help, and you have plenty of energy—far more than I ever had—and so fond of dancing too; and there are so few dances in Redborough. Oh, yes, I think it is a capital plan, Ellen! and Hester will be delighted to help you. It will be such an opening for her," Mrs. John said, with tears of pleasure in her eyes.

Hester did not say much while the talk ran on. She was understood to fall into the scheme, and that was all that was necessary. But when Ellen, after a prolonged visit and a detailed explanation to Mrs. John, which she received with the greatest excitement and interest, of all her arrangements as to the music, the suppers, and every other particular they could think of between them, rose to take her leave, she put her hand within Hester's arm, and drew her aside for a few confidential words.

"Don't think of coming to the door," she said to Mrs. John; "it is so cold you must not stir. Hester will see me out. There is one thing I must say to you, dear," she added, raising herself to Hester's ear when they were out of the mother's hearing, "and you are not to take it amiss. It must be a condition beforehand—now please, Hester, mind, and don't be offended. You must promise me that you will have nothing to say to either of the boys."

The quick flush of offence sprang to Hester's face.

"I don't know what you mean. You mean something you have no right to say, Ellen!"

"I have a very good right to say it—for I'm a married lady, and you are only a girl, and of course I must know best. You are not to have anything to say to the boys. Any one else you like. I am sure I don't mind, but will do anything I can to help—but not the boys. Oh, I know something about Harry. I know you have had the sense to— — Well, I don't understand how far it went, but I suppose it must have gone as far as it could go, for he's not clever enough to be put off with anything less than a real No. But you may have changed your mind, or a hundred things might happen. And then there's Edward; Aunt Catherine would be wild if anything got up between you and Edward. Oh, I think it's always best to speak plain, and then one has nothing to reproach one's self with after. She would just be *wild*, you know. She thinks there is nobody good enough for him; and you and she have never got on. Oh, I don't suppose there's anything between you and Edward. I never said so; the only thing is you must promise me to have nothing to say to *them*. There are plenty of others—much better matches, and more eligible: and it's always a pity to have anything to say to a cousin in that way. You're sure to set the family by the ears; and then it narrows the connection, and you keep always the same name; and there are ever so many drawbacks. So just you promise me, Hester, there's a dear—never," said Ellen, seizing her with both hands, and giving her a sudden perfumy kiss, "never!" and the salute was repeated on the other cheek, "to have *anything* to say to the boys— —"

"The boys! if you think I care anything for the boys! I shall have nothing to say to anybody," cried Hester, with indignation, drawing herself out of this too urgent embrace. Ellen tossed back all her bracelets, and shook her golden locks and her sealskin hat, and made an agitation in the air of scent and sound and movement.

"Oh, that's being a great deal too good," she cried.

Hester stood at the door, and looked on while Mrs. Algernon got into her victoria and drew the fur rug over her, and was driven away, waving the hand and the bracelets in a parting jingle. The girl was not envious, but half-contemptuous, feeling herself in her poverty as much superior to this butterfly in furs and feathers, as pride could desire. Hester did little credit to the social gifts, or the popularity or reputed cleverness in her own way, of her gay cousin who had been the inspiration of Harry, and now was the guide of Algernon Merridew. She said to herself with the downrightness of youth, that Ellen was a little fool. But her own cheeks were blazing with this parting dart which had been thrown at her. The boys! She had a softened feeling of amity towards Harry, who had done all a stupid young man could do to overcome the sentence of disapproval under which Hester was aware she lay. It had been embarrassing and uncomfortable, and had made her anything but grateful at the moment; but now she began to feel that Harry had indeed behaved like a man, and done all that a man could to remedy her false position, and give her a substantial foundation for the native indomitable pride which none of them could crush, though they did their best. No; she would have nothing to say to Harry. She shook her head to herself, and laughed at the thought, all in the silence of the verandah, where she stood hazily gazing out through the dim greenish glass at Ellen, long after Ellen had disappeared. But Edward! that was a different matter altogether. She would give no word so far as he was concerned. Edward was altogether different from Harry. He piqued and excited her curiosity; he kept her mind in a tremor of interest. She could not cease thinking of him when she was in his neighbourhood, wondering what he would do, what he would say. And if it did make Catherine *wild*, as Ellen said, that was but an inducement the more in Hester's indignant soul. She had no wish to please Catherine Vernon. There had not been any love lost between them from the first, and Hester was glad to think she was not one of those who had in any way pretended to her kinswoman's favour. She had never sought Catherine, never bowed the knee before her. When she went to the Grange it had been against her will, as a matter of obedience to her mother, not to Catherine. If it made Catherine wild to think that there was a friendship, or any other sentiment between Edward and the girl whom she had so slighted, then let Catherine be wild. That was no motive to restrain Hester's freedom of action. All this passed through her mind as she stood in the verandah in the cold, gazing after Ellen, long after Ellen was out of sight. There were many things which gave her a sort of attraction of repulsion to Edward. He had tried to deceive Roland Ashton about her, telling him she was about to marry Harry, when he knew very well she had refused to marry Harry. Why had he done it? And in his manner to herself Edward was two men. When they were alone he was more than friendly; he was tender, insinuating, anxious for her approval, eager to unfold himself to her. But when he saw her in the Grange drawing-room he never went near her. In early times she had asked why, and he had answered with deceiving words, asking how she thought he could bear to approach her with commonplace civilities when she was the only creature in the place for whom he cared at all, a speech which had pleased Hester at first as something high-flown and splendid, but which had not preserved its effect as time went on: for she could not see why he should not be civil, and show some regard for her presence, even if he could not devote himself to her. And why could he not devote himself to her? Because it would displease Catherine. When Catherine was not present, there was nobody for him but Hester. When Catherine was there, he was unconscious of her existence. This, of course, should have shown clearly to Hester that he was not worthy of her regard, and to some degree did so. But the conviction was mingled with so lively a curiosity in respect to him, so strong an opposition as regarded her, that Hester's moral judgment was confused altogether. She was anxious, eager to overcome her adversary, excited to know what Edward's meaning was. He would not stand up for her like a true friend, but at the same time he would never let her alone, he would still let her see that she was in his mind. She disliked him, yet—— She almost loved him, but still—— Nothing could be more tantalising, more entirely unlike indifference. To think of meeting Edward in society, yet not under Catherine's eye, made her heart beat loudly. She had never done this hitherto. She had met him by chance on the Common or in the country roads about, and his voice had been almost that of a lover. She had met him before the world, and he had scarcely seemed to know her. But how could these meetings test what he meant? This it was that made Ellen's proposal exciting, even while she herself half scorned it. Harry? no! Poor Harry! she would not disturb his peace, nor say a word, nor even look a look which should put him in jeopardy. But Edward?—ah! that was a different matter. It was with all the vehemence of a quarrel that she snatched at the chance put into her hands, even when she had seemed to scorn it. To know what he meant—to know what was his real state of mind. If he would be afraid of what the world would say, as well as of what Catherine would say—in that case there was no scorn which Hester did not feel herself capable of pouring out upon her unworthy admirer; but if things proved different? Ah! then she did not know what softening, what yielding, she might not be capable of. The very thought melted her heart.

And yet she had thought herself more "interested" (this was what she called it) in Roland Ashton than in any man whom she had ever heard of before. The world had seemed all blank to her when he went away. His step at the door had made her heart thrill: the commonplace day had brightened up into something smiling and sweet when he came in. But then she had not been fighting a duel with him half her life as she had been doing with

Edward. She was not curious, *intriguée*, to know what Roland meant. She thought (with a blush) that she did know—more or less—what he meant. But Edward was a sort of sphinx; he was an enemy to be beaten, a riddle to be read. She said to herself, what would please her best would be to force him into self-abandonment, to carry him so out of himself that he should give up all pretences and own himself at her disposal, and then to turn her back upon him and scorn him. Would she have done so? she thought she would, and that in this lay the secret of her interest in Edward and his crooked ways. And now, here was the trial approaching. She would see what was his true mettle, she would be able indeed to judge of him now.

"Hester," said Mrs. John appearing at the open door, "what do you mean by lingering in the cold, to get your death? You will be chilled to your very bones. You have not even a shawl on, and in this cold place. What are you doing? I have called you three times, and you never paid any attention. Even to stand here for five minutes freezes me."

"Then don't stand here, mamma," said Hester, taking hold of her mother's arm and thus leading her back in the old way. They did not walk about very much together now. Hester preferred her own thoughts to her mother's society, and Mrs. John was not sorry to be left quietly by herself at the fireside. How long it seemed since the time when she held her mother's arm clasped in hers whenever she moved, and used it as a helm to guide that timid and trustful woman wherever she would! A little compunction came over her as she made use of that well-known expedient again, and steered her mother (all the more gently for that thought) back to her own chair.

"Yes, yes, dear, this is very comfortable," said Mrs. John, "but I wish you had come at once, when I called you, for we must not lose any time in thinking about your dresses. You must do Ellen credit, that is one thing clear. I can't have you dowdy, Hester. The Merridew girls shall not have a word to say about the Vernons on your account. Oh, I know they will if they can; they will whisper and say how proud we all are, and give ourselves airs, and just look at Hester in a washed muslin! I would rather go without my dinner," said Mrs. John with vehemence, "for a whole year."

"But I shall not let you do that, mamma."

"Oh, Hester, just hold your tongue. What do you know about it? I would rather sell my Indian shawl, or my pearls—Dear me, what a good thing I did not part with my pearls! that is something nobody can turn up their noses at. And you can say you got them from your mother, and your grandmother before her—which is more than they ever had. But there are the dresses to be thought of," said the tender mother, looking in Hester's face, half awed, half appealing: for even in the pride of descent she was forced to remember that you cannot send your child to a *Thé Dansante* with nothing but a string of pearls round her neck, however fine, and however long in the family it may have been.

"Dresses! one will do," said Hester, with a little flush of pleasure, yet determination to repress her mother's unnecessary liberality. "You forget what you are talking of, mother dear. One dress is as much as— —"

"And to whom do you suppose you are speaking," said Mrs. John with dignity; "there are a great many things which you think you know better than I. Perhaps you are wrong there too; but I am not going to bandy words with you. One thing I must say, than when we talk of ball dresses I know a great deal better than you. Oh, but I do—I had to get everything for myself in old days. Your father delighted in seeing me fine, but he never pretended to have any taste. All the responsibility was on me. Considering that we are poor, and that you are so young, I should think tulle would do: or even tarlatan. Hester, I should like you to have silk slips, that gives a character to a thing at once. A white one, a pink one, and a blue one— —"

"Dear mamma, a white frock, that is all I want. I am sure that is all I want; we can't afford any more. And as for silk slips— —"

"Oh, hold your tongue, Hester, what do you know about it?" cried Mrs. John, exasperated. "You have never been at a ball in your life. You can't know what's wanted, like me. There are quantities of other things besides. Shoes—you must have satin shoes and silk stockings, and gloves, and something to wear in your hair. I don't even know what's worn now. We used to have wreaths in my day, but perhaps that's not the fashion at present. When I had not a maid—and of course, poor child, you have no maid—I used to have a hair-dresser to do my hair when I was going out. We wore it quite high on the top of our heads, and now you wear it down in the nape of your neck. What a thing fashion is! We had gigot sleeves all puffed out with feather cushions, and I used to wear a lace scarf which was very becoming. We had muslins in my time, nice clear book-muslins, and when you had worn it two or three times for balls you just wore it out in the evenings at home. Tarlatan is not half so profitable," said Mrs. John, with a very serious face, "but you must have it, I suppose, all the same."

"Mother," said Hester, when her mother paused for breath, "I feel quite horrified at all this. Why should I dress up so fine for Ellen's parties? I shall only be a sort of poor relation. My washed muslin will do very well. Nobody will expect anything better from me."

"Then that is just why you shall have something better," said the poor lady, her pale countenance brightening with a pretty pink flush. "You sha'n't go at all if you can't go as my daughter should. You shall have a white first, and then a—no, not a pink; pink used to be my colour, for you know I was pale, and my hair was plain brown, not like yours. Yours is a little too—auburn—for pink. You must have a blue for your second, with silk slips made very simply, and tarlatan over that. White shoes, and white gloves, and my pearls. Oh, how glad I am I kept my pearls! It will be such a pleasure, dear, to see you dressed, it will be like old times again. And you must ask Ellen what to wear in your hair, a wreath, or just one flower at the side, with a spray hanging down over your neck. Mr. Ashton, I am sure, would get it for me in town. For flowers and those sort of things one should always send to London. And you must have a fan. I wonder if my ivory fan would be old-fashioned? I must ask Ellen. And, dear child, don't stand there doing nothing when there is not a moment to lose, but ring for the tea. We must have tea first. I always feel better after, and then we must put everything down upon paper, and calculate what it will cost, and how we are to do."

"I don't want all that," said Hester again: but the sound of it flattered her youthful ears; for she was only a girl, when all was said.

"Don't talk any nonsense, child, but ring for the tea," said Mrs. John, feeling herself for once mistress of the occasion. "But Hester," she added, in so solemn a tone that Hester came back half frightened to hear what it was, "if you ever have children, as I hope you will, be sure you have one of your girls taught how to cut out, and to look after the dressmaking. If we only could have them made at home, what a saving it would be!"

CHAPTER VII
THE FIRST OF THEM

Young Mrs. Merridew's *Thés Dansantes* made a great commotion in Redborough. Dancing teas—what did it mean? It meant some nonsense or another. You might be sure it meant nonsense of some kind, as it was Ellen Vernon that was at the bottom of it, the elder people said; but the younger ones were of a different opinion. It did not matter to them so much that Ellen Vernon was silly; indeed the greater part of them were so dazzled by the furs and the bracelets, and the victoria, if not by the brilliant fairness and beaming smiles and prettiness of the bride, that they did not remember Ellen Vernon had been silly, and thought Mrs. Algernon Merridew not only the leader of fashion, but the most amiable and good-natured of all queens of society, the most "easy to get on with" and most full of "go." Nothing like her and her dresses, and her house and her company, had ever been seen in the quiet, steady-going country town. She made it known graciously, that she was always at home at lunch, and there was scarcely a day that a merry party did not assemble at her house, filling the newly-furnished pretty room with chatter and laughter, and all the distracting devices of careless youth to get rid of a few of its golden hours. And already there had been half a dozen dinners, far too soon and quite unnecessary, as all the elders said. She ought to have waited until everybody had given her and her husband a dinner before she began to return their hospitalities. But Ellen had no idea either of waiting or returning the heavy dinners to which she, as a daughter of one of the reigning houses of the town, and her husband as belonging, if not to that rank, at least to the foremost respectability, were invited by all the principal people. The entertainments she gave were reckless young dinners, where there was no solemnity at all, and perhaps not much wit, but where laughter abounded and all sorts of wild schemes of pleasure were invented. And just as the solid people who had made a point of having a dinner for the Algernon Merridews began to feel a little offended at the goings-on of the young household which paid no attention to ordinary rules of civility, the younger portion of the population was thrown into the wildest excitement by the announcement of the *Thés Dansantes*, and frowning mothers were courted to smiles again, by the anticipated pleasure of their children. The old Merridews, the father and mother, looked on with pride but misgiving, the brothers and sisters with pride and delight, as they felt themselves already rising high upon the topmost wave of society by means of their brilliant sister-in-law.

"Only mind what you are about and keep hold on the reins, my boy," old Merridew said to his son, which Algernon promised with a laughing "Trust me for that."

"Trust Algy, indeed!" his mother said, shaking her head. "I would not trust him a step further that I saw him with that crazy little thing by the side of him; all my hope is that being a Vernon her people will step in." They were all sure that no great harm could happen to a Vernon in Redborough. Harry, her brother, was always at her side, as faithful as her husband, backing her up. And Catherine herself could not disapprove, for she went to the house now and then, and laughed when she was spoken to on the subject. "Ellen was always like that," she said, "wild for pleasure and amusement. She has asked me to her dancing teas, as an entertainment quite suited to my years and habits." All which things reassured the Merridews and the other anxious persons about.

"And you are going to this dancing tea?" Catherine Vernon said.

"I suppose so," said Edward, indifferently. "They would think it strange if I did not go. And they expect you—Merridew told me so. He said it would add such dignity to their little party!"

There was something in the tone with which Edward said this which Catherine did not like. It was true that she herself had always represented the invitation as ludicrous, yet it was quite true that her presence would have added dignity to the party, and there was nothing ridiculous in the idea that Algernon Merridew thought so. This annoyed her a little, but it was the annoyance of a moment. She said, "I hope you will enjoy yourself," with a laugh, which Edward on his side found as offensive: but he did not betray this, and smiled in reply, as he knew she meant him to smile, with a sort of apologetic indulgent air.

"I shall do the best I can," he said, and they both laughed. She tenderly, thinking how good he was to take this trouble in order to gratify the frivolous young pair and keep up the Vernon traditions; he with a fierce question to herself, why shouldn't he enjoy it? at least it would be an evening to himself, with nobody to keep watch over him and make a note of every girl he danced with. Alas for Catherine! if she noticed the girls he danced with it was in order to invite them afterwards (if she approved of them), for she had no jealous desire to keep him to herself, but wanted him to marry. But then there was one at least whom she could never have tolerated. And the chief point in Edward's anticipations, as in Hester's, was the freedom of intercourse permitted under Ellen's easy young wing, and the opportunity he would have of seeing how the eager, large-eyed girl would look among other girls, when he could approach her freely. This gave him something of the same sense of curiosity which was so warm in Hester's mind. How would she look among other girls—how would she receive him? It did not occur to him as probable that she would resent that avoidance of her when under Catherine's eye which he had so often assured her made him wretched. He felt that the little secret between them, the stolen glance he would give her at the Grange parties, the little shrug with which he pointed her attention to his bondage, would have an attraction even greater than had he been always at her side; and in some sense this was true. But he did not think of Hester's judgment and of the natural indignation of her high spirit; neither did he think of the comparison she made between him and Harry, who had never hesitated to show his devotion. To compare himself and Harry, seemed to Edward impossible. A big idiot—a nonentity. She had more sense than that.

Never was there such a spectacle seen in Redborough as the first of the *Thés Dansantes*. The Merridews' house was near the White House, and consequently on a little eminence, which answered all the purposes of a great eminence in that flat country. It stood in the midst of a little shrubbery above which it rose on white steps, to make the position still more commanding. There was a long domed conservatory at one side, the windows were all plate glass, and when you consider that within and without the place was lighted up—like the Crystal Palace, people said—you may imagine something of the imposing effect. The conservatory was all hung with Chinese lanterns, and was fairy land to the young guests inexperienced in such glorious effects; the two drawing-rooms were both thrown open for dancing. There were very few chaperons; only here and there a middle-aged mother, too devoted to her charge, yawned behind her fan with nobody to speak to, not a lady of her own age to exchange experiences with, no elderly gallant to get her a cup of tea. All was youth, rampant, insolent, careless—feeling that the world was made for it, and rejoicing to shake itself free of every trammel. Mrs. Ellen set them the example in the most daring way.

"What do we want with the old things here?" she said; "they would much rather be in bed, and the best place for them. I don't suppose you mean to do anything wrong, any of you girls, and if you did they wouldn't stop you. If you can't take care of yourselves, if you want a chaperon, there's me. And there's Fanny Willoughby, and Lilian Melville, and Maud Seton; they've all been married as long as I have. Where could you find steadier married women? and ain't we enough to chaperon a couple of dozen girls? I never pretend to ask old people, unless it was just to let them see how everything looks, poor old things, once in a way."

This being the creed of the mistress of the feast, it is not to be supposed that her disciples were more catholic. And there was no limit to the fun which the young people promised themselves. To do them justice, it was very innocent fun. The greatest sin on the conscience of the wildest romp in the place was that of having danced ten times with a favourite partner, besides sitting out all the square dances (of which there were only two) in his company. Algernon himself had insisted upon two. He said it was respectable: and he danced both with the least popular of the young ladies, that they might not feel themselves slighted, for he was a very good fellow.

"Did you ever see such a muff?" his wife said, who never condescended to the Lancers. "I do believe he likes to hop about with the ugliest thing he can pick up. I thought I had kept out all the ugly girls, but I haven't succeeded. If there is one, Algy is sure to find her out."

"To show you that you have no need to be jealous," some one said.

"Oh, *jealous*!" cried Ellen, with supreme disdain.

The young Merridews, brothers and sisters, thought her the most wonderful creature that had ever been born. Her light hair was in curls and frizzes (newly come in and extremely captivating) all over her head. Her dress was a sort of purple, a colour nobody but herself ventured to wear, but which threw up her fairness with the most brilliant effect. She had all her jewellery on, from the diamonds Harry had spent all his available money (under her own directions) in buying for her, to the little bracelet contributed by the clerks at the bank. Her arm was covered nearly up to the elbow, and the sound she made when they fell over her hands and she had to push them back again was wonderful. It was like a whole concert of fairy music, the bangles representing the higher notes, the big golden manacles furnishing a bass. She liked to hold up her hands and shake them back with a pretty cry of "Tiresome! Why is one forced to wear all this upon one?" Ellen said.

And Mrs. John had accomplished her wish. She had got, if not three, at least two new dresses for Hester, one upon her shoulders at this moment, the other, the blue one, laid up all ready in the box. White of course was the first. It had the silk slip upon which Mrs. John had set her heart, which was so much more thrifty than anything else, which could be covered over again and again, as she pointed out to her daughter, and which at the present moment was veiled in floods and billows of tarlatan. Tarlatan was the fashion of those days: anything that was limp, that took—as people now love to say, "nice folds," being considered utterly dowdy. And when Hester appeared in those crisp puffings, with her pearls round her throat, and white flowers in the hair which her mother called auburn, even young Mrs. Merridew herself held her breath. She turned her cousin round and round to examine her.

"Well, I call that a *beautiful* dress," she said. "Who put it into your head to get a dress like that? Why, it is the height of the fashion! Those *bouillonées* are just the right thing to wear. And do you mean to say these are real pearls? Oh, go away, or I shall kill you! Why have I not pearls? They are far more *distingués*—oh, far more!—than my paltry bits of diamonds. Oh, take her away, or I shall not be able to keep my hands off her. And such flowers! they must have come from Forster's. I am certain they came from Forster's. Mine are French, but they are not so pretty," Ellen said.

Hester stood and smiled while these comments were made, though with a half sense of shame. She thought it annoyed her very much to be subjected to such a survey, and so no doubt it would have done had not the result been so satisfactory; but it is hard to be really displeased by approbation.

As for Ellen, she whispered behind her hand to Harry, "The old lady must have a great deal more than we think for. She must have been saving up. You don't get a dress like that for nothing."

"It's not the dress—she always looks nice, whatever she puts on," said faithful Harry.

His sister contemplated him with eyes full of contempt. "What is the use of talking to such a silly?" she said. "Not the dress! She never looked one ten-thousandth part so well all her life, and that you know just as well as me."

No, she had never looked so well all her nineteen years. Her dress was simple indeed, but it was perfect in all its details, for Mrs. John had remembered everything. The flowers were artificial, which also was the fashion then, but they were from Forster's, procured by Roland Ashton and brought down by his sister Emma, who had arrived that same afternoon. The pearls were beautiful, more beautiful than any other ornament in the room. Hester stood beside her cousin to receive the guests with a sense that there were no imperfections about her. In the days of the washed muslin there was always a fear that the flounces were not quite even, the bows were not quite firmly sewed on, or something else which at any moment might come to pieces and betray the homemadeness of the garment. But she stood up in her virgin robes with a sense of delightful security—a knowledge that all was complete, which was exhilarating to her spirits. She was not the one white swan in this little provincial party: there were faces quite as lovely as Hester's, which, as a matter of fact, was not so perfect as her dress; but there was no one to whom the anticipated pleasure was so entirely ideal. Her mind did not come down to practical delights at all. She was going to be happy—was she going to be happy? How does it feel to be happy? These were the questions in her mind. She had been so, she was aware, as children are, without knowing it; but this would be conscious, whatever it was.

The dancing began. It was a very pretty scene, and Hester, not in herself perhaps so overwhelmingly gay as the others about her, was caught upon that stream of careless youth and carried with it in spite of herself. An atmosphere of pleasure was about her; eyes looked upon her admiring, almost caressing, every glance was pleasant; the rougher part of the world had disappeared altogether. It was as if there was nothing but merry dancers, laughing engagements, an interchange of enjoyment, all about. Happy! Well, she could not say that this was not happiness. It might be so, for anything she could tell. There was not much that was ideal about it, but yet—. Just as she was thinking this, she felt in a moment of repose her hand suddenly taken, drawn into some one else's hand: and, looking round suddenly, saw Edward close to her, looking at her with a subdued glow in his eyes, a look of admiration and wonder. It was quite a steady, straightforward gaze—not furtive, not flying. She started at the touch and look, and attempted to draw away her hand, but it was held fast. But he had not lifted her hand, he had taken it where it hung half-veiled by her furbelows, and he had turned his back towards the company isolating her in a corner, while he inspected her. He drew a long breath apparently of satisfaction and pleasure.

"I am late," he said, "but this was worth waiting for. Cinderella, where have you left your pumpkin coach?"

Hester's brow grew dark, her heart seemed to swoon away in her bosom altogether, then came to itself again with a rush of heat and indignation. She wrenched her hand out of that hold, a flood of colour came to her cheeks.

"I suppose you mean to insult me," she said; "but this is not a place to insult me—I am among friends here."

"Why do you say so, Hester? Insult you! What an ungenerous thing to say! as if I was in the habit of doing so, and must not here because you have friends. What a cruel thing to say!"

"Would you rather have it in your power to insult me always?" said Hester. Her lip began to quiver a little. What an odious thing it is to be a woman, to be always ready, when you would rather not, when you want to show yourself most strong and angry, to cry! She clenched her hands tightly to keep herself down. "I am no cinder-wench, Mr. Edward Vernon," she said. "I have given you no reason to call me so. It is a pitiful thing for a man to notice a girl's dress. If I am dressed poorly, I am not ashamed of it. It is not a sin to be poor."

"Hester! a girl of your sense to be so foolish! How could I mean that? What I meant was, that you have come out glorious, like the moon from the clouds. Nothing could be sweeter than that little house-frock you used to wear out on the Common. I liked it better than all the finery. But to-night you are like a young princess. Why did I say Cinderella? Heaven knows; just because I was dazzled and bewildered, and because you are a princess; and the pleasure of seeing you made my head go round. Have I made my peace? Well then, there's a darling, turn round and let me see you, that I may see all the finery, and everything that makes you so lovely, in detail."

"You may have made it a little better," said Hester; "but why do you go on talking like that? I am neither lovely nor a darling; and you shall not say so—you! that would not see me if this, instead of being Ellen's house, were the Grange."

"You have me at your mercy there," said Edward. "I confess you have me at your mercy, there."

Upon which Hester melted a little, and, perceiving the abashed look which he had put on, began to falter, and presently found herself guilty of the commonplace expedient of asking if he did not think it a pretty scene.

"Oh, very pretty," said Edward; "that is to say, I don't know anything about it. I looked for one individual when I came in, and as, as soon as I found her, she began to bully me violently, I feel a little muddled, and I don't know what to think. Give me a little time."

By this time, as was natural, Hester began to think herself a monster of folly and unkindness, and to feel that she was ready to sink through the floor with shame.

"I did not mean to be cross," she said. "I thought—that is, I had been looking—that is——"

Here she stopped, feeling herself get deeper and deeper into difficulty. Her countenance changed from the girlish freshness of complexion, which everybody admired, into a burning red; her eyelids unable to keep up, her heart beating as if it would burst through silk slip, and tarlatan *bouillonée*, and all——

"Come, let us have this dance. I like the music," said Edward, drawing her hand suddenly through his arm.

"But I am engaged."

"Oh, never mind, if you are engaged. You were engaged to me before ever you came," he said, lightly, and drew her into the whirl. Hester was at the age (in society), when, to throw over a partner, looks like the guiltiest treachery. She could not take any pleasure in the dance, for thought of it.

"I must go and ask his pardon. I am sure I am very sorry. I did not intend to be so false; and there he is, poor man, not dancing."

These words Hester said breathless over the shoulder of the enterprising intruder, who had carried her off under the victim's eyes.

"Poor man!" Edward echoed, with a laugh. "I am glad he has nobody to dance with. What right had he to engage you? and you regret him; and you don't want me."

Here Hester rebuked her cousin.

"You have no right to say so. I might want—I mean I might like very well to dance with you when you condescended to ask me; but not to be run away with, without a word, and made to do a false thing. False things are what I hate."

"You say that with such meaning. You must be thinking of more than a dance. Am I one of the false things you hate?"

"I do not hate you," said Hester, as they came to a pause, looking doubtfully into his face; "but I do not think you are very true."

"You mean I don't blurt out everything I mean, and am capable now and then of keeping something to myself. I can keep my own counsel—not like that fellow there," Edward permitted himself to say: which was a mistake; for Hester looked up and saw the gaze of honest Harry dwelling upon her with some regret, and much tenderness, and was touched at once with sympathy and indignation.

"If you mean Harry, no one could ever doubt *him*," said Hester, in the warmth of her compunction. "If he is your friend, he is always your friend. He is not afraid of what any one says."

"Ah, Hester, you are always harping on that string," said Edward. "I know what you mean; but can't you understand the position I am in, and understand *me*? Don't you know I am in bondage? I cannot say my soul is my own. I dare not think nor feel but as I am told. If I were to follow my own heart without disguise, I think it would be my ruin. We will not name any names, but you know. And I know what you think about that big stupid there, but you are mistaken. It is not that his heart is more true. It is that he has not brains enough to see what is liked and what is not liked. He is not even sympathetic enough. He does what he likes, and never considers if it is good for him or not."

"Sympathetic!" cried Hester. "He is sympathetic with me. When he sees me lonely and neglected he comes and stands beside me. If he cannot do more, he does do that. I don't pretend to say that he is very amusing," she continued, with a laugh, "but he does what he can. He stands by me. Oh! failing other things that are better, I like that. Rather than being sympathetic with Catherine, I like him to sympathise with me."

"There is no question of names," said Edward, "We must not get personal. But I am glad you find Harry amusing. I never heard that he was so before. He is standing by Ellen now; that's what he's here for. They will come to grief, these young people. They are beginning a great deal too fast. You know young Merridew, or old Merridew either, can never keep up this. Ellen ought to know better. But Harry will have scope for this great accomplishment that you appreciate so highly. He will have to stand by his sister."

"And he will," Hester said.

She scarcely thought of the dancing, so much did this conversation—so unlike a conversation to be carried on in the whirl of a waltz—occupy her. It occurred to her now, as breath failed her, to remember how in all the accounts of a first ball she had ever read, the heroine had felt all other sentiments melt away in the rapturous pleasure of dancing with the man of her heart. Novels were all Hester's experience. She remembered this, and it gave her a half comic, half miserable sensation to realise that she was not thinking about the dancing at all. She was carrying on her duel with Edward. There was always a warm sense of gratification in that—a stirring up of all her faculties. She liked to go on carrying it a step further, defying and puzzling him, and wondering on his side how much he meant, how much that he left to be inferred, was true. The heroine in a novel is generally the point of everybody's admiration in the ball-room, and to look at the perfection of the waltz which she and her lover enjoy so deeply, the whole assemblage stands still. But nothing of this kind occurred in Hester's case. As she had so little experience, the chances are that she was by no means the best dancer in the room, and certainly Edward was not the other best. Their waltz was the means of carrying on the discussion which to both was the most attractive possibility. When she realised this, Hester was a little amused, but likewise a good deal disappointed. She felt a disagreeable limit thus placed to her power to enjoy.

"Come into the conservatory," Edward said. "Don't you think you have had enough? Oh, it is your first ball. I suppose you like it; but I am beginning to lose my relish for those sort of affairs."

"You are not so old that you should give up dancing, Cousin Edward."

"Old! No, I hope I am not old yet, and I don't intend to give up dancing; but I like to walk here better—with you. I like to talk better—with you. I like to see your face, Hester, and see how it changes from kindness to wrath, from friendship to indignation, from a patient sense that I am endurable, to a violent consciousness—— Come and sit here."

"You seem to think I never do anything but think of you: and that is the greatest mistake," Hester said.

Upon which he laughed. The place he had led her to was only partially lighted. There were many other groups scattered about among the plants and stands of flowers. Flirtation was openly recognised in this youthful house as one of the portions of the evening's entertainment, and large provision made for it. There was nobody to notice with whom it was that Edward was amusing himself, and he felt fully disposed to take advantage of his opportunities. He laughed at Hester's indignant disclosures. "If you did not think a little about me, dear, you would not notice so distinctly my course of conduct in other places, you could not be sure that it was much more agreeable to me, instead of standing by your side and trying to be as amusing as Harry, to lead down Mrs. Houseman and old Lady Kearney to supper or to tea."

"My mother should go out of the room before either of them," cried Hester. "Do you know who she is? Sir John Westwood is her cousin: a duke's daughter once married into her family——"

"I quite understand you and agree with you, Hester. It is nothing that she is a perfect little gentlewoman, and has far better manners than any of us; but because she is a cousin to a heavy baronet, who is not good enough to tie her shoe——"

"Edward!" The girl was so startled she could not believe her ears.

"Oh, I know very well what I am saying. You don't know me, that is all. You think I am a natural snob, when I am only a snob by circumstances. You yourself, Hester, do you really think your mother should stand upon her cousin and upon Lady Ethelinda (or whatever was her name), her great-grandmother, and not upon herself far better than either? I can't imagine you think that."

Hester was surprised and silenced for the moment. She had been so often reminded of the noble grandmother and the baronet cousin, and so hard put to it to find a ground of superiority on which her pride could take refuge, that this sudden appeal to her better judgment bewildered her. She was startled to find those advantages which were indisputable, and to which everybody deferred in theory, so boldly under-valued; but yet the manner of doing it made her heart beat with pleasure. Yes; people thought her dear little mother silly, and Hester was aware that she was not clever. Sometimes, in the depths of her own soul, she had chafed, as children will, at the poor lady's dulness and slowness of comprehension; but she *was* a perfect little gentlewoman. And he saw it! He felt in his heart that she was above them all—not because of Lady Ethelinda (she was Lady Sarah in reality) and Sir John, but herself.

"I did not know you were a Radical," she said. She knew nothing about Radicals, though instinctively in her heart she agreed with them. "I thought you cared for family and that sort of thing."

"Do you?"

Hester paused. She flung higher her young head, which was proud with life and a sense of power unknown. "I should like to be a king's daughter," she said, "or a great soldier's or a great statesman's. I should like my name to mean something. I should like people to say, when they hear it, that is— —"

"But you don't care much about Sir John?—that is what I thought. I am no Radical; I am all for decorum and established order and church and state. How could you doubt that? But, by the way, there is a person whom neither of us like, who certainly has the kind of rank you prize. Don't you know who I mean, Hester? When a stranger comes to Redborough, there is one name he is sure to hear. If she were a duchess she could not be better known. To be her relation carries a certain weight. We were always a leading family in the place, I suppose. But why are we, for instance, so much better than the Merridews and all the rest of the respectable people? She has something to do with it, I can't deny, though I don't like her any more than you."

"Edward," cried Hester breathlessly, "about that we ought to understand each other. I have no reason to like Catherine. Yes, I will say her name; why shouldn't I? She has not liked me. I was only a child, and if I was saucy she might have forgiven me, all these years. But she has taken the trouble on the contrary to humiliate me, to make me feel that I am nobody, which was unworthy. But you: she has been kind to you. She has been more than kind—she has loved you. I have seen it in her eyes. She thinks that nobody is worth thinking of in comparison with you. If—if—who shall I say?—if Sir Walter Scott came here, or Mr. Tennyson, she would rather have you. And yet, you that ought to be so grateful, that ought to love her back, that ought to be proud—oh, I should if I were you. If she were fond of me I should be proud. I hate all those wretched people who take from her hand, and then sneer and snarl at her, like dogs—no, not like dogs: dogs are far nobler—like cats; that is better."

Hester's eyes were shining with eloquence and ardour; the little movement of her head so proud, so animated, so full of visionary passion, threw back and gave a certain freedom to the hair which her mother called auburn. Her whole figure was full of that force and meaning which is above beauty. Edward looked at her with smiling admiration. If his conscience was touched, or his temper at least, he did not show it.

"Do you call me a cat?" he said.

"Oh, I am not in fun. I am as earnest as ever I can be. It is wicked, it is miserable, and I cannot understand you. All the others are as nothing in comparison with you."

He grew a little pale under this accusation; he would not meet it directly. "But you know," he said, "why she hates you. It is for your mother's sake."

"My mother!" cried Hester astonished. "But no one could hate my mother." The suggestion took away her breath.

"It is true, all the same. I thought you did not know. She was to have married John Vernon, your father, and he preferred——that is the whole account of it; then he got into trouble, and she had her revenge."

"Did she ruin my father?" said Hester in a low whisper of horror.

"I—don't know if it went so far as that," Edward said.

A hesitation was in his speech. It was scarcely compunction, but doubt, lest a statement of this kind, so easily to be contradicted, might be injudicious on his part—but then, who would speak to Hester on such a subject? And her mother was a little fool, and, most likely, did not know, or would be sure to mistake, the circumstances.

"Don't let us talk of that: it is so long past," he said; "and here is a wretch, a scoundrel, coming up with his eye fixed upon you as if he was a partner. How I loathe all your partners, Hester! Mind, the rest of the dances are for me. I shall watch for you as soon as you have shaken that fellow off."

But Hester did not care for the dances that followed. She went through them indifferently, faithful to the partners who had presented themselves before he came on the scene; and, indeed, the conversation in the conservatory had not drawn her nearer to Edward. It had given her a great deal to think of. She had not time in the whirl and fluster of this gaiety to think it all out.

CHAPTER VIII
A NEW COMPETITOR

Emma Ashton had brought Hester's flowers, and though she was tired with her journey, had taken a great deal of interest in Hester's dress. When she came in to show herself to the old people in her white robes before her ball, the stranger had surveyed her with much attention. She had kissed her slowly and deliberately when introduced to her.

"Roland told me a great deal about you," she said. "I suppose we are cousins too. You look very nice. I hope you will enjoy yourself." She was a very deliberate, measured talker, doing everything steadily. When Hester was gone, she resumed her seat beside her grandmother.

"Roland admires her very much. She is pretty, but I should think she had a great deal of temper," Emma said.

"Temper is scarcely the word. She is a great favourite with your grandfather—and with me too—with me too."

"Roland told me," said Emma. "When I say temper I don't mean any harm. She would do much better for Roland if she had a good deal of temper. That is what he wants to keep him straight; for a man ought not to flirt after he is married, and he will, unless she keeps him in order."

"Married! but is he likely to marry? I did not hear anything of it."

"When a man can keep a sister he can keep a wife," said Emma, announcing this fact as if it were an oracle. "He has a house, and everything that is necessary. And of course I shall not stand in his way. I can go back to Elinor, where I am a sort of head nurse, and cheap enough at the money; or I can be a governess. That touches his pride—he does not like that."

Here the old captain came back, who had been putting his favourite carefully into the fly.

"Why has she not her mother with her?" he said. "I like a girl to have her mother with her. It is pretty, it is natural. I do not like those new-fashioned, independent ways."

"But they are much more convenient, grandpapa," said Emma. "Think how I should have been situated had a girl always wanted her mother with her. Elinor, with her family, cannot always be going out; and when she goes she likes to amuse herself, she does not go for me. A girl going out with her mother means a devoted sort of old lady like the mothers in books. Such nonsense, you know—for a girl's mother, when she is eighteen or so, is rarely more than forty, and people of forty like amusement just as much as we do. It is better, on the whole, I think, when every one is for herself."

"Well, that is not my opinion," said the old captain, shortly.

He was accustomed to do most of the talking himself, and it startled him to have it thus taken out of his hand.

"I suppose an invitation will come for me," said Emma calmly, "as soon as they know I am here; and then Hester and I can go together. Roland said there was no dancing, but I think it always safest to bring a ball-dress. It is not heavy, though it takes up a good deal of room; but then you can always take one box into the carriage, and the railway only charges by weight."

"Roland is very busy, I suppose, my dear. You only see him in the evening?"

"I don't always see him in the evening. He has his own friends, and I am getting a few acquaintances too. If he gives me my living and very little to do I ought to be grateful to him, but I would not let him give up his own amusements for me. That wouldn't be fair. Oh yes, he is very busy. He has found so many new people to do business for down here."

"I hope to goodness he won't speculate with their money and ruin them," Captain Morgan said.

"Ruin! oh, I hope not. But Roland says there is nothing so exciting as to be on the verge of ruin. He says it is better than a play: for instead of looking on at the acting, the acting is going on inside of you. But it is his trade to speculate, isn't it, grandpapa? That is what he is there for, and he is very good at it they say. I suppose this girl has not any money? When they are pretty and nice they seldom have."

"What girl?" said Captain Morgan, almost haughtily—as haughtily and harshly as the old gentleman could persuade himself to speak.

"Doesn't he know, grandmamma?" said Emma, "the girl Roland admired so much: and she would just do for him, if she had some money: but so nice looking as he is, and so well established in business, I don't think, unless there is money, he should throw himself away."

"Is it Hester Vernon that you mean?" asked the captain in an angry voice.

"She does not mean any harm, Rowley. Don't you see Hester is just to her an abstract person, not the dear girl she is to you and me. And Emma," said the old lady almost with timidity, "I fear your ball-dress will not be of much use. Mrs. Merridew will not think of inviting you—she will not perhaps know you are here."

"Roland met her, grandmamma," said Emma calmly. "He told me; we are all cousins, I believe. She will be sure to invite me, or if not, you will be able to get me an invitation. People always exert themselves to get invitations for girls. It is like helping young men on in business. We cannot go and make acquaintances for ourselves as young men go and set up offices, but we must have our chance, you know, as well. Of course," said Emma in her deliberate way, "it is for everybody's advantage that we should have our chance as well as the men."

"And what do you call your chance?" said Captain Morgan. He planted himself in the front of the fireplace with his legs very wide apart, which, as his wife well understood, meant war.

"My old man," she said, "what do you know about the talk of girls? They have one way of thinking, and we have another. They are young, and we are old."

"Hester is younger than she is," said the captain, "let her alone. She is as ready to talk as there is any need to be."

"My chance, grandpapa?" said Emma with a slow little laugh. "It is not necessary, is it, to explain? a girl's chance is in making—friends. If one goes for a governess one's family does not like it. They would rather you were your sister's head nurse with all the trouble, and without any pay. Roland has taken me now—and I do not require to work for my living; but it is not so very cheerful with Roland that I should not wish—if I could—to make a change. We must all think of ourselves you know."

"My dear," said the old lady in her soft voice, "in one way that is very true."

"It is very true, I think, in every way. It might be cheerful for me if Roland were to spend his evenings at home as Tom Pinch in Dickens did with his sister. But then Roland is not a bit like Tom Pinch, and I said to him when I came, 'You are not to change your life for me.' So that sometimes, you know, I am in the house all alone all day, and then if he is out to dinner, or if he has any evening engagement, I am alone all the night. And if he were to marry, why there would be an end of me altogether. So you see, grandmamma, wherever I am, it is very natural that I should wish to have my chance."

"How old are you?" said the captain abruptly.

"I shall be twenty-three at Christmas," said Emma, raising her eyes to his face. She was curious to know why he asked—whether he thought her older, or younger than her age, whether he thought it was strange she should still be unmarried. "I was kept very much out of sight when I was with Elinor," she said half apologetically. She had not had her "chance" as she had always wished to have. She had not been very well treated she felt in this life, the youngest of seven. She had been passed on from one to another of her married sisters to make herself useful. All of them had said that Emma must "come out," but no one had taken any trouble about it. She had to scramble for a dress, a very cheap one, and to coax Elinor into taking her to some little local merrymaking, and so opening, as it were, the gates of society. As soon as she could say that she was "out" Emma had kept the idea of having "her chance" of making friends and getting invitations always before her. But her opportunities had not been great, and Elinor had not devoted herself to her younger sister. She was still young enough to amuse herself, and it had not occurred to her to put so unimportant a person as Emma in the foreground. So that she had never been allowed to have much of a "chance." Emma had not much experience of the world. Of the many novels she had read, and which were her guides to life, a great many devoted themselves to the history and description of young ladies at whose entrance into a ball-room every man present fell metaphorically on his knees. She was acquainted with many evening parties in fiction at which the fate of countless young men and women was decided. The smallest dance would be represented there as bringing people together who were never more to be sundered. Emma herself had not produced any such sensation at the small parties she had hitherto gone to, but she felt that this glory must be awaiting her, and especially that in a new place like this Redborough, in some waltz or other, among some unknown assembly she should meet her fate.

This being the case, it is not to be wondered at that she should lose no time in announcing her certainty of an invitation to anything so likely to conduce to such an object as Ellen Merridew's dancing teas. She had come down to Redborough prepared to be cousin to all the world. Roland, indeed, had taken pains to explain that Catherine Vernon's cousins were not actually *her* cousins, but she had thought it better in many ways to ignore this, and to descend upon the new scene with the most amiable disposition to embrace as a near relative every Vernon presented to her. Among them all, what could be more likely than that her fate should be found? She meant no harm to anybody. It would be doing no harm, certainly, if any young man fell in love with her, to make him happy by marrying him. She felt most strongly the supreme necessity of marrying for her own part. She had no disguise with herself on this subject, and with her grandparents she did not think it necessary to have any disguise. Everything was involved in it. Roland had taken the responsibility of her upon himself and given her a home, with very little to do, and enough to make her sufficiently comfortable. Emma had always been brought up to consider everything from a strictly practical point of view. She had been taught to believe that she had no right to anything, that it was out of their bounty and charity that her brothers and sisters, now one, now another, afforded her a temporary home. And she was very comfortable with Roland—but if he were to marry, what then? The comfort of having a home of her own, a husband of her own with a settled income, was to Emma in prospect the crown of all good things. She would not have been ashamed to say so if necessary; and it was in balls and parties and picnics and social meetings generally, that a young woman had her chance of suddenly obtaining, by looking pretty, by making herself agreeable, all these good things at a stroke. She made up her mind at once that heaven and earth must be moved to get her an invitation to Mrs. Algernon Merridew's *Thés Dansantes*. She would not take, she said to herself, any denial. She would see all the Redborough people there, among whom there must certainly be some individuals of the class upon which depended Emma's fate. As she sat unfolding so much of this as was needful with a calm confidence in being understood, her grandparents, with a sort of stupefaction, listened and looked on. Emma was knitting all the time in the German way, with a very slight swift movement of her fingers and without looking at her work. She spoke slowly, with an air of such undoubted fact and practical commonplace about her, that those two old people, who each in their several ways indulged in fancy and sentiment, were daunted and silenced. Emma spoke in a sort of saintly simplicity, as not knowing that anything beyond those solid primitive foundations, anything like sentiment or fancy, was in the world.

She was not handsome like her brother, and yet there was something remarkable about her appearance which some people admired. Her hair was dark, her features sufficiently good. The strange thing in her was her eyes, which were very light in colour—so light, that sometimes there seemed no colour at all in them. This was not beautiful, but it was *bizarre* and unusual, and as such Emma had her admirers. But it was only in this particular, not in mind or thoughts, that there was anything in her out of the way.

"Well?" said the old captain to his wife, when, after having yawned softly over her work as a signal and preparation for bed-going, Emma rose with a smile at half-past ten, and kissed them both, and asked if she might have her candle. "I must not keep you out of bed," she said, with that look of complacent consideration which, notwithstanding, was quite innocent and referred to her own circumscribed horizon, in which everything connected with herself was well in the foreground. Mrs. Morgan did not meet her husband's eye as she had met it when Roland was the visitor.

"She has not been well brought up, poor thing!" the old lady said. "She has had no one to care for her—and, Rowley, she is our own flesh and blood."

"That's the wonderful thing," the captain said, "Katie's child! My dear, I give it up; there seems no reason and no sense in it. I cannot think what the Lord can mean."

"Oh, hush, Rowley—nothing, nothing that is not good."

"One would say—that there must be just a crowd of souls ready to put into the new little bodies, and that one must slip down before the other that ought to come;—like that vile cad, you know, that slipped into the pool of Siloam before the poor fellow that had no servant could shuffle down."

"And that was all the better for your poor fellow as it turned out, Rowley, for he got his healing more sweetly out of the very hand—— And, poor little spirit, if it was not intended for this body, I can't think it has got very much by its deceit," Mrs. Morgan said, with a little laugh.

But the captain did not laugh. There was consternation in his soul.

"A girl," he said, "with her eyes open to all chances, looking out for a husband, and seriously thinking that is the right thing to do—to come from you and me, Mary—to come from you and me!"

The old lady gave him her hands that he might help her out of her chair, and when she stood upright, tottering a little—for she was not strong upon her legs—she gave him a little playful tap with her finger upon his old cheek.

"You are just a high-flown old sentimentalist," she said. "There is no harm in her. She is only prose to your poetry—which I've always been all our lives, and you've said so many a day."

"Don't blaspheme, old woman, don't blaspheme," the captain said.

But next day, when Hester came in to give them the account—which she knew the old people would expect—of all that had happened, Emma lost no time in making her desires known.

"It must have been a very pretty party," she said; "a conservatory lighted like that is always so nice. It is cool to sit in after you have got heated with dancing. I wish I could have seen you all enjoying yourselves. I am so fond of dancing, and I don't get much; for Roland does not care for dancing parties, and at Waltham Elinor never had time. I suppose you had an invitation, grandmamma, though you are too old to go?"

Here Hester explained, wondering, that there were very few chaperons, and nobody asked but people who were known to dance.

"Ellen says it only tires the others, and what is the use?" Hester said.

"That is very true; she must be judicious—she must have right notions. When do you think my invitation will come, grandmamma? I suppose people will call when they know I am here?"

Here there was a little pause, for even Mrs. Morgan was taken aback by this question, and did not know what to say.

"I am sure," said Hester blushing, after a minute's silence, "that if Miss Ashton would—like it so very much——"

"Oh, I should, of course, *very* much. I want to know the Redborough people. I like to know the people wherever I go. It is so dull knowing no one," Emma said. "And then it would be so convenient, you know, for I could go with—you——"

To this Hester did not know what to reply; but it was well in one way that the new comer took it all for granted and gave no trouble. Emma made no account of embarrassed looks and hesitating replies. She did not even notice them, but pursued her own way deliberately, impervious to any discouragement, which was more equivocal than a flat "No." She had been used to "noes" very flat and uncompromising, and everything less seemed to her to mean assent. When she had disposed, as she thought, of this question, she went on to another which was of still greater importance.

"But I cannot expect Cousin Catherine to call upon me," she said composedly. "She is too old, and she is always treated as a kind of princess, Roland says. And you are too old to take me, grandmamma. Perhaps I could go with Hester. Would that be the right thing? For they all say I must not neglect Cousin Catherine."

Hester looked aghast upon the young woman, who contemplated them so calmly over her knitting, and talked of neglecting Catherine, and being called upon by the sovereign of society, who left even the Redborough magnates out, and called only upon those who pleased her. Emma went on quite placidly, knitting with the ends of her fingers in that phlegmatic German way, which is an offence to English knitters. The stocking went on dropping in longer and longer lengths from her hands, as if twirling upon a leisurely wheel. She had explained that they were knickerbocker stockings, for Elinor's boys, which she was always busy with.

"She gives me so much for them, for every dozen pairs—and the wool; I make a little by it, and it is much cheaper for her than the shops."

"Your grandfather will take you—some day," said Mrs. Morgan hastily.

"Oh, that will do very well, but it ought to be soon," Emma said. She returned to the subject after Hester had given a further account of the merrymaking of the previous night.

"Are you all great friends?" said Emma, "or are there little factions as there generally are in families? Elinor and William's wife used always to be having tiffs, and then the rest of us had to take sides. I never would. I thought it was wisest not. I was nobody, you know, only the youngest. And when one has to stay a few months here and a few months there, without any home of one's own, it is best to keep out of all these quarrels, don't you think, grandmamma? Roland said there were some old things living here, some old maids that were spiteful."

Now it is curious enough that though the Miss Vernon-Ridgways were not at all approved by their neighbours, it gave these ladies a shock to hear an outsider describe them thus.

"Never mind that," said Mrs. Morgan, almost impatiently. "Are you going further, Hester? If you want my old man, tell him not to stay out too long, for the wind is cold to-day."

"I am going to Redborough," Hester said. "I have some things to do for mamma."

"Oh, you must take me with you," said Emma—"just one moment till I have turned this heel. I never like to leave a heel midway. I want to see Redborough of all things. Grandmamma, you will not mind me leaving you—I want to see all I can, as I don't know how long I may stay."

"Do you mind, Hester?" the old lady said in a little alarm, as having finished the heel, and put her knitting carefully away in a long basket made to hold the length of her needles, Emma went up stairs to get her hat. Hester laughed a little and hesitated, for though she was not moved to enthusiasm by Emma, she was young enough to like the novelty of a new companion, whoever that might be.

"I hope she will not make me take her to see Catherine. Catherine would not be very gracious to any one whom I brought her. Dear Mrs. Morgan, I wanted to ask you—Was Catherine——Did Catherine——"

"What, my dear?"

"Nothing—I can't tell you before any one. It was something I heard from——last night. Yes, I am quite ready, Miss Ashton," Hester said.

"It is grand to be called Miss Ashton, but I wish you would say Emma. It makes me feel as if I were some one's governess when you say Miss Ashton. I nearly was," said Emma. "You know we are a large family, eight of us, and we had no money. I am sure I can't tell how we managed to grow up. It was thanks to Elinor I believe; she was the only one who could manage papa. And now they are all provided for, but only me. Elinor and Bee made very good marriages, and Kate didn't do so badly either, but she's gone to India. The others were to help me between them, but that is not very nice. They are always scheming to have as little of you as they can, and to make the others have too much. I never would give in to that. I always kept to my day. I used to say 'No, Bee, my time is up. I don't mind where you put me (for I never made any fuss in that sort of way, it turns the servants against you), I can sleep anywhere, but you must keep your turn. Elinor sha'n't be put upon if I can help it,' and the short and the long of it was that I had as nearly as possible taken a governess's place."

"That would have been better surely—to be independent," Hester said.

"In some ways. To have a paid salary would be very nice—but it hurts a girl's chance. Oh, yes, it does," said Emma, "there is no doubt of it: people say not when they want to coax you into it, but it does—and as all the others have married so well, of course I was very unwilling to do anything to damage my chance."

"What was your chance?" said Hester with a set countenance: partly she did not know, and partly from the context she divined, and meant to crush her companion with lofty indignation: but Emma was not quick enough to perceive the moral disapproval. She was not even conscious that it was possible to disapprove of such an elemental necessity.

"Oh, you know very well," she said with a little laugh. "I have never been a flirt. I haven't got any inclination that way. Of course in my position I would think it my duty to consider any offer. But I was very nearly driven to the governessing," she continued calmly. "Elinor had visitors coming, and Bee was so ill-natured as to start painting and papering just as I was due there. Can you imagine anything more nasty? just to be able to say she could not take me in! I just said I must take a situation, and they were in a way. But I do really believe I should have done it had it not been for Roland. He said it would suit him very well to have me. He had just got a house of his own, you know, and I could be of use to him. So he took me, which was very kind. It is a little dull after being used to children, but I have scarcely anything to do, and he gives me a little allowance for my clothes. Don't you think it is very kind?"

"I would much rather be a governess," Hester said with a glow of indignant pride. This matter-of-fact description of the state of dependence, which was made without any sense of injury at all, with the composure of an individual fully capable of holding her own and looking for nothing else, had an effect upon her sensitive mind which it is impossible to describe. She shrank from the revelation as if it had been something terrible; and yet it was not terrible at all, but the most calm historic account of a state of affairs which seemed perfectly natural to every one concerned. Emma knew that she would herself have employed any possible expedient to get rid of an unnecessary member of her household, especially such a detrimental as "the youngest"—and she was not angry with Bee.

"Ah, you don't know children," said Emma serenely. "I have been used to them all my life, and I know what demons they are; and then it does so spoil your chances in life. Being with Roland is very nice you know, he never orders me about, and he gives me an allowance for my clothes, as I told you. But it is much duller. At Elinor's and Bee's, and even at William's, there's a little life going on. Now and then you can't help seeing people. Even when your sisters don't wish it, people will ask you out when they know you're there. And I must say that for Elinor, that when she's not worried she does take a little trouble about you, and always likes to see you look nice. To be sure with five boys and a husband in business, she is worried," Emma added with impartiality, "most of the time. What is that big house, that red one, so near the road? Nice people ought to live there."

"That is the Grange," said Hester, with a sudden flush, "that is Catherine Vernon's house."

"Oh—h! But then why should I lose any time? It would look better that I should go at once, the very first day. I suppose you run in whenever you please."

Hester's countenance flamed more than ever. "I never go—except when I go with my mother. Catherine would not care to see you with me. She is very fond of your grandfather and grandmother—but not so fond of us. And she is quite right, we don't deserve it so much," Hester said, flinging back her young head with that movement of natural pride which belonged to her. Just then, to make the situation more complicated, Edward came out from the gate, and seeing the two figures on the road, hesitated for a moment, conscious of Catherine's eye behind him, and Hester's keen consciousness before.

"Oh," said Emma again, "then there *are* factions? I am sure I am very glad grandpapa is on Catherine's side; for Elinor said, and then Roland told me—— Who is that? Oh, then, there are *men* there? I thought she lived alone. He looks rather nice, though I like men to be taller than that. Mind you introduce me, and walk a little faster please, before he gets away."

Hester's response to this was naturally the indignant one of walking more slowly, so as to give the hesitating figure at the gate full time to get away. But Edward had thought better of it. On the whole, he found it more undesirable to encounter Hester's disdain than anything Catherine would be likely to say. And just at that hour after luncheon Catherine generally abandoned her seat in the window. It was true that he very seldom came back to lunch. He advanced accordingly a few steps from the door, and held out his hand. "I am glad to see you are none the worse of our dissipations last night," he said.

"Introduce me," said Emma, keeping her place close to Hester's side, "we are all cousins together, though we don't know each other. I wanted to go in at once to see Cousin Catherine, whom I have heard of all my life; but she will not let me. Perhaps you will mention it to Cousin Catherine. I will come as soon as I can get grandpapa to bring me. It is so much more formal than I thought. Among relations generally one runs out and in, and never thinks twice, but that does not seem to be your way here."

"No, it is not our way here. We hold each other at arm's length. We are not even civil if we can help it," said Edward, with a laugh and a glance at Hester, who stood, the impersonation of unwilling politeness, holding herself back, in an attitude which said as plainly as words, that though their way was the same she did not choose to be accompanied, by him, along even that common way.

"I see," said Emma. "I am sure I am very sorry I made you stand and talk, Hester, when you dislike it so much. Of course, among relations one understands all that. Do you live here? I remember now Roland told me there were some gentlemen-cousins, but I am quite a stranger, and I don't know anything. Hester is going to take me to see the little town."

"You must not say 'little town' to any of the Redborough people, Miss Ashton."

"Oh, mustn't I? At Waltham nobody minds. I should like to see the Bank where all the Vernon money comes from. The Vernon money has never done us any good I believe, but still when one is connected with money one likes to see all about it at least. Do you think, Hester, this gentleman would be so good as to see about my invitation? I don't know if Mrs. ——, I forget her name, who gives the dances—is your sister, Mr. Vernon."

"Mrs. Merridew is my cousin," said Edward.

"Oh, cousin, is it? I suppose we are all cousins. Naturally I should like an invitation: but I suppose it is because of the splits in the family, grandmamma doesn't seem to wish to do anything about it, and Hester hesitated, you know, just as you hesitated, Mr. Vernon, before you came to speak to us. What a pity that there should be such to-does: but where there are a large number of people in a family, of course it can't always be helped. I have always found gentlemen were more good-natured than ladies about getting one invitations. If you were to tell Mrs. Merridew I am here, even if she didn't think it right to call as most people would, at least she might send me a ticket. I can't have anything to do with either side, seeing I only arrived yesterday, and don't know a word about it: but I do like to make acquaintance with a place wherever I go."

"I will see that my cousin sends you an invitation, Miss Ashton, at least if she will do what I ask her. I have got my work waiting me. Pardon me if I go on."

"Oh, we are going the same way. I suppose we are going the same way?" said Emma, looking at her companion.

"You walk quicker than we do, and I dare say you are in a hurry," said Hester ungraciously. She did not respond to the look of mingled reproach and relief which he gave her. The very vicinity of Catherine Vernon's house stiffened Hester into marble, and Edward was very anxious to go on. He stood still for one moment with his hat in his hand, then hastened on, at a rate very little like his usual mode of progression. Hester on her part followed with studious lingering, pausing to point out to her companion the view over the Common, the roofs of the Redborough houses, the White House on the opposite slope. Emma naturally conceived her own suspicions from this curious piece of pantomime. They had been walking smartly before, they walked slowly now—and hers was what she thought a romantic imagination. She felt confident that these two were true lovers separated by some family squabble, and that they did not venture to be seen walking together. "I know we were going the same way," she said, "because there are not two ways, and you can see the town before you. I can't see why we might not have walked together. It is sinful to carry family tiffs so far," Emma said.

CHAPTER IX
A DOUBLE MIND

Edward had drawn his bow at a venture when he made that statement about Catherine to Hester, and he was full of doubt as to how it would influence her. This was the first time almost that he had disregarded opinion and withdrawn the bolts and bars and let himself go. There was something in the atmosphere of the young house, all breathing of life and freedom, and daring disregard of all trammels, which got into his head in spite of himself. He had abandoned altogether the decorous habits of his life, the necessity which bound him as surely in a dance as at his office. On ordinary occasions, wherever a ball occurred in Redborough, Edward was aware beforehand which young ladies he would have to dance with, and knew that he must apportion his attentions rightly, and neglect nobody whose father or mother had been civil to him. He knew that he must not dance too often with one, nor sit out in corners, nor do anything unbecoming a young man upon whom the eyes of many were fixed. But the very air in the house of the Merridews was different from that of other places. There was a licence in it which existed nowhere else. He, the staid and grave, carried off Hester from her partners, appropriated her for a good part of the evening, sat with her hidden away among the ferns in the conservatory, and only resigned her when he was compelled to do so. Even then, by way of emphasising his choice of Hester, he scarcely danced at all after, but stood among the other disengaged men in the doorways, watching her and seizing every opportunity to gain her attention. He was startled at himself when he thought of it. He walked home in the middle of the night, in the faint wintry moonlight, following the old fly he heard lumbering off in the distance carrying her home, his mind filled with a curious excitement and sense of self-abandonment. He had always admired her—her independence, her courage, her eager intelligence, had furnished him since she was a child with a sort of ideal. He had kept wondering what kind of woman she would grow up; and lo! here she was, a woman grown, drawing other eyes than his, the object of admiring glances and complimentary remarks. When he had seen her in her washed muslin at Catherine Vernon's parties, she had still appeared to him a child, or little more than a child. He had still felt the superiority of his own position, and that the passing glance and shrug of familiar confidential half-apology would probably please her more than the ordinary attentions which he had to show among so many. But Hester, by Ellen Merridew's side, a taller and grander woman, well-dressed, with her mother's pearls about her white throat, which was as white as they, was a different creature altogether. To risk everything for a mere school-girl was one thing, but a stately young creature like this, at whom everybody looked, of whom everybody said, "*That* Hester Vernon? Dear me, I never thought she had grown up like that!" was a different matter. The sight of her had intoxicated Edward. Perhaps poor Mrs. John's pearls and the careful perfection of her dress had something to do with it. And the place intoxicated him. There every one was doing what seemed good in his own sight. There were few or none of those stern reminders which he had read elsewhere in the eyes of parents whose daughters were waiting to be danced with, the "Was-it-for-this-I-asked-you-to-dinner?" look, to which he had so often succumbed. For once he had lost his head; he was even vaguely conscious that he had come there with a sort of intention of losing his head, and for once thinking of his own pleasure, and nothing more. No doubt this had been in his mind: and the sudden sight of that white figure, all graceful and stately, and of Mrs. John's pearls, had done the rest. But he was a little nervous next morning as he thought over what he had been doing; he did not bear Catherine's questioning well at breakfast. When she asked him whom he had danced with, he made answer that he had danced very little. But yet he had enjoyed himself, oh yes. It had been so pretty a party that it had been pleasure enough to look on. He described the conservatory and its Chinese lanterns with enthusiasm. "It must, indeed, have been like fairyland—or the fireworks at the Crystal Palace," Catherine had said. And he had felt a bitter pang of offence, as she laughed. He did not feel, indeed, that he could bear any remarks of the kind, or depreciation of Ellen, for whom he felt a special kindness just now. When Catherine said, "But all this must have come to a great deal of money: Algernon Merridew has only a share in his father's business, he has no private money, has he?—but, of course I know he has no private means: and Ellen's little money will soon go at that rate."

"I don't suppose Chinese lanterns cost very much," said Edward.

"Your temper is doubtful this morning," said Catherine, with a smile. "It is 'on the go,' which is usual enough after late hours and the excitement of a dance; but I don't think you are often so much excited by a dance. Did you see some one whom you admired, Edward? I am sure, if she is a nice girl, I shall be very glad."

"Perhaps it would be as well not to try, Aunt Catherine; we might not agree about what a nice girl is."

"No?" said Catherine rather wistfully.

She looked into his doubtful eyes across the breakfast table, and, perhaps for the first time, began to feel that she was not so very certain as she had once been as to what her boy meant. Was it possible after all, that perhaps the words upon which they agreed had different meanings to each? But this was only a passing cloud.

"Who was the belle?" she said smiling; "you can tell me that, at least, if you can't tell who you admired most."

Edward paused; and then an impulse of audacity seized him.

"I don't know if you will like it," he said, "but if I must tell the truth, I think that girl at the Vernonry—Hester, you know, who is grown up, it appears, and *out*—"

Catherine bore the little shock with great self-possession, but she felt it.

"Hester. Why should you suppose I would not like it? She must be nineteen, and, of course, she is *out*. And what of her?" Catherine said, with a grave smile.

She was vexed that Edward should be the one to tell her of the girl's success, and she was vexed, too, that he should think it would displease her. Why should it displease her? He ought to have kept silence on the subject, and he ought not to have seemed to know that she had any feeling upon it: the suggestion hurt her pride.

"Ellen seems to have taken her up. She has grown up much handsomer than I should have expected, and she was very well dressed, with beautiful pearls— —"

"Ah!" said Catherine, with a long breath; "then her mother kept her pearls!" She laughed a moment after, and added, "Of course, she would; what could I have expected? She kept her settlement. Poor little thing! I suppose she did not understand what it meant, and that she was cheating her husband's creditors."

"I never quite understood," said Edward, "why you should have brought her here, and given her a house, when she is still in possession of that income."

"She has only a scrap of it. Poor little thing! She neither knew it was wrong to take it, nor that if she did keep it, it ought not to have been allowed to go for his after debts. She got muddled altogether among them. The greater part of it she mortgaged for him, so that there was only a pittance left. Whatever you may think, you young men, it is a drawback for a man when he marries a fool. And so she kept her pearls!" Catherine added, with a laugh of contempt.

"Marrying a fool, however, must have its advantages," said Edward, "since a woman with brains would probably have given up the settlement altogether."

"Advantages—if you think them advantages!" Catherine said, with a flash of her eyes such as Edward had seldom seen. "And certainly would not have kept the pearls—which are worth a good deal of money," she added, however, with her habitual laugh. "I think they must have dazzled you, my boy, these pearls."

"I am sure they did," said Edward composedly; "they took away my breath. I have seen her here often, a dowdy little girl" (he scorned himself for saying these words, yet he said them, though even his cheek reddened with the sense of self-contempt) "with no ornaments at all."

"No," said Catherine; "to do Mrs. John justice, she had as much sense as that. She would not have put those pearls on a girl's neck, unless she was dressed conformably. Oh, she has sense enough for that. I suppose she had a pretty dress—white? But of course it would be white; at the first ball—and looked well, you say?"

"Very handsome," said Edward, gravely. He did not look up to meet the look of awakened alarm, wonder, doubt, and rousing up of her faculties to meet a new danger, which was in Catherine's eyes. He kept his on his plate and ate his breakfast with great apparent calm, though he knew very well, and had pleasure in thinking, that he had planted an arrow in her. "By the way," he said, after an interval, "where did John Vernon pick his wife up? I hear she is of good family—and was it her extravagance that brought about his ruin? These are details I have never heard."

"It is not necessary to enter into such old stories," said Catherine, somewhat stiffly. "He met her, I suppose, as young men meet unsuitable people everywhere; but we must do justice. I don't think she had any share in the ruin, any more at least than a woman's legitimate share," she added, with a laugh that was somewhat grim. "He was fond of every kind of indulgence, and then speculated to mend matters. Beware of speculation, Edward. Extravagance is bad, but speculation is ruin. In the one case you may have to buy your pleasures very dear, but in the other there is no pleasure, nothing but destruction and misery."

"Is not that a little hard, Aunt Catherine? there is another side to it. Sometimes a colossal fortune instead of destruction, as you say; and in the meantime a great deal of excitement and interest, which are pleasures in their way."

"The pleasure of balancing on the point of a needle over the bottomless pit," she said. "If I were not very sure that you have too much sense to be drawn into anything of the kind, I should take fright, to hear you say even as much as that. The very name of speculation is a horror to me."

"Yet there must always be a little of it in business," he said, with a smile creeping about the corners of his mouth.

"You think me old-fashioned in my notions, and with a woman's incapacity to understand business; but in my day we managed to do very well without it," Catherine said.

"To think of a woman's incapacity for business in your presence would be silly indeed. I hope I am not such an ass as that," said Edward, looking up at her with a smile. And she thought his look so kind and true, so full of affectionate filial admiration and trust, that Catherine's keen perceptions were of no more use to her than the foolishness of any mother.

He returned to luncheon that day as if for the purpose of obliterating all disagreeable impressions, and it was on leaving the Grange to return to the bank that he met Hester and Emma. This confused and annoyed him for the moment. It was not so that he would have liked to meet the heroine of last night; and her unknown companion, and the highly inappropriate place of meeting, made the encounter still less to his taste. But when he had hurried on in advance he began to ask himself what was the meaning of Hester's reluctance to walk with him, or even to speak to him, her attitude—drawing back even from his greeting, and the clouded look in her eyes. It was natural that he should not wish to speak to her at the door of the Grange, but why she should wish to avoid him he could not tell. It would have been a triumph over Catherine to have thus demonstrated her acquaintance with him at Catherine's very door. So Edward thought, having only the vulgar conception of feminine enmity. On the whole, seeing that he had sowed the seeds of suspicion in Catherine's bosom, it was better that Hester should hold him at arm's length. Yet he was piqued by it. When he reached the bank, however, news awaited him, which turned his thoughts in a different channel. He found Harry Vernon and Algernon Merridew in great excitement in the room which was sacred to the former. Ashton had made the first *coup* on their behalf. He had bought in for them, at a fabulously low price, certain stock by which in a few weeks he was confident they might almost double their ventures. To furnish the details of this operation is beyond the writer's power, but the three young men understood it, or thought they understood it. Of course a skilful buyer prowling about a crowded market with real money in his pocket, knowing what he wants, and what is profitable, will be likely to get his money's worth, whether he is buying potatoes or stock.

"I saw it was very low," said Merridew, "and wondered at the time if Ashton would be down upon it. I thought of writing to him, but on the whole I suppose it's best not to cramp them in their operations. They ought to know their own business best."

"They shell it out when there's a good thing going, these fellows do," said Harry, out of his moustache.

"And nobody has any money apparently," Algernon said, with a laugh of pleasure, meaning to imply *save you and me*. "When money's tight, that is the time to place a little with advantage," he said with a profound air. "I think you should go in for it on a larger scale, you two fellows that have the command of the bank."

"I wouldn't risk too much at once," Harry said.

Edward listened to their prattle with a contempt which almost reached the length of passion. To hear them talk as if they understood, or as if it mattered what they thought! His own brains were swelling with excitement. He knew that he could go a great deal further if he pleased, and that Harry's share in the decision would be small. Dancing on the point of a needle over the bottomless pit! It was like an old woman's insane objection to anything daring—anything out of the common way. Ashton's letter to him was far longer and more detailed than his communications with the others. He said plainly that here was an opportunity for an operation really upon a grand scale, and that there could be no doubt of a dazzling success. "You will communicate just as much or as little of this as you think proper to the others," Roland wrote, and it was all that Edward could do to keep up an appearance of replying to them, of joining in their gratification as he pondered this much more important proposal. "It is not once in a dozen years that such a chance arises," Roland said.

Now Edward had nothing of his own to speak of, far less than the others, who each had a trifle of independent fortune. All that he could risk was the money of the bank. The profit, if profit there was, would be to the bank, and even that large increase of profit would have its drawbacks, for Catherine, who liked to know everything, would inquire into it, and in her opinion, success would be scarcely less dangerous than failure. He could not stop in the drab-coloured calm of the office where these two young idiots were congratulating each other, and trying to talk as if they knew all about it. His scorn of them was unspeakable. If they gained a hundred pounds their elation would be boundless. They were like boys sending out a little toy frigate and enchanted when it reached in safety the opposite side of the puddle. But Ashton meant business. It was not for this sort of trifling work that he had set himself to watch those fluctuations, which are more delicate than anything in nature they could be compared to. The blowing of the winds and their changes were prose compared to the headlong poetry of the money-market. Edward felt so many new pulses waking in him, such a hurrying fever in his veins, that he could not control himself.

"You'll be here, I suppose, Harry, till closing time? I'm going out," he said.

"You going out—you that never have anything to do out of doors! I had to umpire in a match on the other side of the Common," said Harry, "but if you'll just tell Cordwainer as you pass to get some one else in my place, I don't mind staying. I'm sure you've done it often, Ned, for me."

"I am not in request, like you; but I have something I want to see to, to-day."

"All right," said Harry. "Don't you go and overdo it, whatever it is."

"You are seedy with staying up, dancing and flirting," said young Merridew, with his imbecile laugh. "Nelly says she could not believe her eyes."

"I wish Ellen, and you too, would understand that dancing and flirting are entirely out of my way," said Edward, with a flush of anger, as he took his hat and went out.

Poor Algernon's innocent joke was doubly unsuccessful, for Harry stood perfectly glum, not moving a muscle. He had not been at all amused by the proceedings of the previous night.

"I wouldn't report it, if I were you, when Ellen says silly things," said her brother, as black as a thunder-cloud.

"By Jove!" said poor Merridew, falling from his eminence of satisfaction into the ludicrous dismay of undeserved depreciation. He told his wife after, "They both set upon me tooth and nail, when I meant nothing but to be pleasant."

"I wish you would learn, Algernon, that it's always wise to hold your tongue when I'm not there," Ellen said. "Of course I understand my own family. And not much wonder they were vexed! Edward that doesn't look at a girl because of Aunt Catherine, and Harry that she has snubbed so! You could not have chosen a worse subject to be pleasant upon," Mrs. Ellen said.

But it was not this subject that was in Edward's mind as he sallied forth with the step and the air of that correct and blameless man of business which already all Redborough believed him to be. He had taken that aspect upon him in the most marvellous way—the air of a man whose mind was balanced like his books, as regularly, and without the variation of a farthing. He was one of those who are born punctual, and already his morning appearance was as a clock to many people on the outskirts of Redborough. His hat, his gloves, his very umbrella, were enough to give people confidence. There was nobody who would have hesitated to entrust their money to his hands. But if Redborough could have known, as he passed along the streets, causing a little wonder to various people—for already it had become a surprising fact that Mr. Edward should leave business at so much earlier an hour than usual—what a wild excitement was passing through Edward's veins, the town would have been soared out of its composure altogether. He scarcely felt the pavement under his feet; he scarcely knew which way he was turning. The message for Cordwainer went out of his head, though he went that way on purpose. Several important questions had come before him to be settled since he had taken his place at the head of the bank. He had been called upon to decide whether here and there an old customer who had not thriven in the world should be allowed to borrow, or a new one permitted to overdraw; and in such cases he had stood upon the security of the bank with a firmness which was invulnerable, and listened to no weak voices of pity. But this was far more important than such questions as these. As his ideas disentangled themselves, there seemed to be two possibilities before him. If he threw himself into Ashton's scheme at all, to do it as a partner in the business, not indeed with the sanction of his other partners, but, if there was risk to the firm in his proceedings at large, to make them profitable to it in case of success. In case of success! Of course there would be success. It was inevitable that they must succeed. On the other side, the expedient was to use the money and the securities of the bank, not for the aggrandisement of Vernon's, but for his own. This would leave the responsibility of the action entirely upon his own shoulders if anything went wrong. And he did not refuse to give a rapid glance at that contingency. What could it mean to the bank? Not ruin—he half-smiled as he thought. It would mean coming down perhaps in the world, descending from the *prestige* and importance of its present rank. And to himself it would mean going to the dogs—anyhow, there could be no doubt on that point. But on the other side! that was better worth looking at, more worthy of consideration. It would be like pouring in new blood to stagnant veins; it would be new life coming in, new energy, something that would stir the old fabric through and through, and stimulate its steady-going, old-fashioned existence. It would be the something he had longed for—the liberating influence, new possibilities, more extended work. He thought, with an excitement that gradually overmastered him, of the rush of gain coming in like a river, and the exhilaration and new force it would bring. This idea caught him up as a strong wind might have caught him, and carried him beyond his own control. He walked faster and faster, skimming along the road that led into the country, into the quiet, where no one could note his altered aspect or the excitement that devoured him, taking off his hat as he got out of sight of the houses, to let the air blow upon his forehead and clear his senses. And by and by things began to become more clear. He read Ashton's letter over again, and with every word the way seemed to grow plainer, the risks less. It was as near a dead certainty as anything could be in business. "Of course there is always a possibility that something unforeseen may happen," Ashton wrote, "and it is for you to weigh this. I think myself that the chance is so infinitesimal as not to be worth taking into consideration; but I would not wish to bias your judgment; the only thing is, that the decision must be immediate." Now that the first shock of novelty was over, he felt it in his power to "weigh this," as Ashton said. Getting familiarised with the subject made him more impartial, he said to himself. The first mention of it had raised a cowardly host of apprehensions and doubts, but now that the throbbing of excitement began to die away, he saw the matter as it was—a question of calculation, a delicate operation, a good *coup*, but all within the legitimate limits of business. He had recovered, he felt, the use of his reason, which the novelty, the necessity for immediate determination, the certainty that he must take no counsel on the subject, that Harry would be dumbly obstinate, and Catherine anxiously, hortatively, immovably against it, had taken away. Harry was an ass, he said to himself, recovering his calm, and Aunt Catherine an old woman. What was the use of the faculties he possessed, and the position he had gained, if in such a crisis he could not act boldly and for himself!

Thus it was with a very different aspect that Edward walked back. He put on his hat, feeling himself cooled and subdued; his pulses returned to their usual rate of beating, which was essentially a moderate one. And so rapidly had he skimmed over the ground, and so quick had been the progress both of his steps and his thoughts, that when he got back, with his mind made up, to the skirts of the Common, he saw the football party just beginning to assemble, and recollected that he had never given Harry's message to Cordwainer, and that accordingly no new umpire could have been found in Harry's place. But what did that matter? He reflected benevolently, with a contemptuous good nature, that he could get back to the bank in time still to liberate his cousin, so that everybody would be satisfied. This he did, stopping at the telegraph office on the way. His despatch was as follows:— "Proceed, but with caution. Needful will be forthcoming." He drew a long breath when he thus decided his fate; then he returned with all the ease and relief which naturally comes with a decision. The thing was done, whether for good or evil—and there could be very little doubt that it was for good. His countenance was cheerful and easy as he returned to the bank.

"I did not give your message, for my business did not keep me so long as I expected. Your football fellows are just collecting. You can get there, if you make haste, before they begin."

"Oh, thanks, awfully!" said Harry. "I hope you did not hurry, though I'm glad to go. I hope you understand I'm always ready to stay, Ned, when you want the time. Of course, you're worth two of me here, I know that; but I can't stand anything that's not fair, and if you want to get away——"

"I don't, old fellow; I've done my business. It did not take so long as I thought. You had better be off if you want to get there in time."

"All right," said Harry. And he went off to his match in a softened state of mind, which, had he been able to divine it, would have astonished Edward greatly. Harry had seen Hester and her companion pass, and he felt a sad conviction that Edward's sudden business had something to do with that apparition. Well! he had said to himself, and what then? Hadn't he a right to try, the same as another? If she liked one better than the other, should the fellow she wouldn't have be such a cad as to stand in her way? This was what had made Harry "fly out," as Algy said, upon his brother-in-law; it had made him pass a very sombre hour alone in the bank. But in the revulsion of feeling at Edward's rapid return, and the likelihood either that he had not seen Hester, or that she would have nothing to say to him, Harry's heart was moved within him. Either his cousin was "in the same box" as himself and rejected, or else he was innocent altogether of evil intention—and in either case Harry's heart was soft to him: at once as one whom he had wronged, and as one who might be suffering with him under a common calamity.

CHAPTER X
STRAIGHTFORWARD

"I hope, Cousin Catherine," said Emma, "that you will not think it is any want of civility on my part. I wished very much to come the first day. I went out with Hester Vernon, who is constantly at grandpapa's—and I was quite distressed, when I found we had to pass here, that she would not bring me in to call. But she seemed to think you would rather not. Of course I know that there are often tiffs in families, so I wouldn't say anything. There are times when Elinor wouldn't call on William's wife not if life and death depended on it; so I understand quite well, and of course a stranger mustn't interfere. Only I wish you to know that I had no wish to take sides, and didn't mean to be rude. That was the last thing in the world I intended. Elinor has always told us younger ones so much about you."

"It is very kind of Elinor, I am sure; and you have behaved most judiciously," said Catherine, with a twinkle in her eye. "It is unnecessary to say to a person of your judgment that in the best regulated family——"

"Oh, you needn't tell me," said Emma, shaking her head. "Nobody can know better than I do. It is very awkward when you are the youngest, and when you are expected by everybody to take their part. Of course they have all been very kind to me. I live part of my time with one, and part with another, and that is why every one thinks I should be on their side. But now I am very independent," Emma said, "for Roland has taken me. I dare say he would tell you, Cousin Catherine, when he was here."

"That must be a very pleasant arrangement," said Catherine, with a smile. "I suppose when you were with Elinor you had a good deal to do."

"I do Roland's housekeeping now. I don't wish to be idle," said Emma. "But to be sure when there are children to be seen after you are never done, and especially boys. Elinor has five boys!—it is something dreadful! The stockings and the mending you can't think! It is very nice being with Roland; he is most kind. He gives me a regular allowance for my clothes, which I never got before, and I am sure it is very good of him; but you can't have everything, you know, and it is a little dull. He is out all day, and often in the evenings, for of course I shouldn't wish him to give up his gentlemen-engagements for me. I don't think people should ever do that sort of thing.

Tom Pinch is all very well in Dickens, but it would be inconvenient in actual life; for suppose you married?—and of course that is what every girl expects to do."

"To be sure," said Catherine. "Is there anything of that sort in prospect, if I may be permitted to ask?"

"Of course, I am quite pleased that you should ask," said Emma. "It would be such a comfort to have somebody like you to come and talk it over with, Cousin Catherine, if there was anything—for I should feel sure you could tell me about my trousseau and all that. But there is nothing, I am sorry to say. You see I have had so little chance. Elinor took me out sometimes, but not much, and she was far more disposed to amuse herself than to introduce me. I don't think that is nice in a married sister, do you? and speaking of that, Cousin Catherine, I am sure you will be kind enough to help me here. Grandpapa will not take any trouble about it. I asked the gentleman whom we met coming out of here, Hester and I—Mr. Edward I think is his name."

"What of Edward?" said Catherine quickly, with a touch of alarm.

"But nothing seems to have come of it," said the persistent Emma. "He said he would try, and Hester made a sort of promise; but there has been one since and I have never been asked. It is your niece's dance—Mrs. Merridew, I think, is her name. She gives one every week, and both for a little amusement, and that I mayn't lose any chance that may be going, I should like very much to go. I don't doubt that you could get me an invitation in a moment if you would just say you would like it."

Catherine's consternation was ludicrous to behold. She was herself so much amused by the situation that she laughed till the tears stood in her eyes. But this matter-of-fact young woman who sat by and gazed upon her with such a stolid incapacity to see the joke, was of the side of the house to which Catherine could pardon anything—the old captain's grandchild, Roland's sister. What would have been vulgar assurance in another, was amusing *naïveté* in Emma. When she had got over her laugh she said, with amused remonstrance as if she had been speaking to a child—

"But you must know, Emma, that these family tiffs you are so well accustomed to, come in to prevent this too. Ellen would not care for my recommendation. She is a very self-willed little person, and indeed the chief rebel of the family."

"That is all very well, Cousin Catherine," said Emma with the downrightness of fact and certainty; "but you know you are the head of the family. You have got the money. If they were in trouble they would all have to come to you: and if you said "I wish this," of course nobody would venture to refuse you. The most stupid person must be sure of that."

There was a commanding commonsense in this view that silenced Catherine. She looked at the young philosopher almost with awe.

"Your arguments are unanswerable," she said; "there is nothing to be said against such admirable logic."

"Then you will ask for an invitation for me?" said Emma. "I am sure I am much obliged to you, Cousin Catherine. It is always best to come to the fountain-head. And it isn't as if I were going to cause any expense or trouble, for I have my ball-dress all ready. I have wore it only once, and it is quite fresh. It is my second ball-dress; the first I wore about a dozen times. Elinor gave it me, which was very kind of her. It was only muslin, but really it was very nice, and got up quite respectably. But this one I bought myself out of the allowance Roland gives me. Don't you think it is very thoughtful of him? for of course what a sister buys for you, however kind she is, is never just the same as what you would choose for yourself."

"I suppose not—I never had any experience," said Catherine, gravely. "I am afraid, however, that you will not meet anybody who will much advance your views at Redborough. It is an old-fashioned, backward place. London would afford a much larger scope for any social operations. Indeed it is very condescending in a young lady from town to give any attention to us and our little parties down here."

"Oh!" said Emma, eager to correct a mistake, "that just shows how little people in the country know. You think London means the London you read of in books, where you meet all the great people and have half-a-dozen parties every night. But when London means Kilburn!" said Emma shaking her head, "where all the gentlemen go to the city every morning, and there is perhaps one dance given in a whole season, and only the people asked that you know! and we know scarcely one. You see the people there don't think of calling because they are your neighbours. There are so many: and unless you get introductions, or work in the parish, or something— Working in the parish is a very good way," Emma added, with a sudden recollection; "you get invited to a great many evening parties where you just stand about and talk, or people sing: and not many dances. Unfortunately I never was much used to parish work. In Elinor's there was too much to do, and Bee was too worldly, and as for William's wife, though we should not like it to be known, Cousin Catherine, she is—a Dissenter."

Emma made this admission with the reluctance it merited.

"I have not told grandpapa," she said, with bated breath.

"I think he could bear it," said Catherine. "I think you might venture on the communication. In some things he is very strong-minded."

"It was a very bitter pill to us," Emma said.

Here they were interrupted by the entrance of the captain himself, who had left his grandchild in a cowardly way to make Catherine's acquaintance by herself. But Emma had not minded. She had not even divined that his pretence of business was hypocritical. She had not been alarmed by Catherine, and now she was comfortably confident of having made a good impression, and secured a friend.

"I am quite ready, grandpapa," she said. "Cousin Catherine has been so kind. She says she will speak to Mrs. Merridew about my invitation, so you may make yourself quite easy on that subject. And grandmamma will be very pleased. Of course I could not expect such an old lady as she is to exert herself. But Cousin Catherine understands how important that sort of thing is to a girl," Emma said, with an air of great gravity.

The captain gave Catherine a piteous glance. He did not understand the new specimen of womankind of whom he had the responsibility, and Catherine, whose powers of self-restraint had been called forth to an unusual degree, responded with an outburst of laughter.

"We have got on admirably," she said. "I like a straightforward mind, with such a power of applying reason to practical uses. You must come to see me often, Emma. Never mind grandpapa. He will tell you I am busy, but when I am so, I shall tell you so. You are far too sensible to take offence."

"Oh, offence, Cousin Catherine? between you and me!" said Emma, "that would be too ridiculous. I hope I know my place. When you are the youngest you soon learn that. Your first lesson is that nobody wants you, and that you must just do the best you can for yourself. There is only just one thing I should like to mention, and that is, that the first time it would be a great advantage to me if you would take me. It is such a fine thing for a girl when she is known to belong to the best people in a place. It is not even as if my name were Vernon. But people will say 'Miss Ashton! who is Miss Ashton? I never heard of her!' Whereas if I were with you, the best partners in the place would ask to get introduced to me, and that would give me a start. Afterwards I could get on by myself, as I hear Mrs. Merridew does not care for chaperons," Emma said.

Once more Catherine was struck dumb. She pushed her chair back a little and regarded this dauntless young woman with a mixture of dismay, admiration, and amusement.

"But I assure you I have never gone to any of Ellen's junketings," she said.

"That will not matter," said the persistent Emma, "Of course she will be pleased to have you. It will be a great honour. And then to me it would be such an advantage. I should feel that I really was having my chance."

When she left the gate of the Grange, walking by the side of the bewildered captain, Emma felt that she was tolerably sure of getting all she wanted, and her triumph, though quite moderate and serious, was great.

"I am very glad you left me to make acquaintance with Cousin Catherine by myself," she said, "grandpapa; I was a little frightened, but she was so nice. She was very nice to Roland too; and it will be such an advantage to go into society for the first time with such a well-known person. It makes all the difference. People see at once who you are, and there is no difficulty afterwards."

"And you think Catherine Vernon will depart from all her habits and take you to that butterfly's ball?" the captain said.

"Of course, grandpapa," said Emma, in the calm of simple conviction. It was not a matter which admitted of any doubt.

And the wonderful thing was, that she proved right. To her own great amazement, and to the consternation of everybody concerned, Catherine Vernon assumed her grey gown, the gayest of her evening garments, and most befitting a dance, and took Emma Ashton in her own carriage to Mrs. Merridew's house on the hill. Catherine was too genial a person in ordinary society to exercise any discouraging influence upon the young party in general; but upon the members of her own family there was no doubt that she did have a subduing effect. Ellen's face of consternation was the subject of remark in the family for years after; indeed, they spoke of "the night when Aunt Catherine came to the dance," dating things from it, as people speak of a great national event. Harry was the one who showed himself most equal to the occasion. He established himself by Catherine's side as a sort of guard of honour, relieving the frightened Algernon, who, what with pride and pleasure on his own part, and a wondering sympathy with Ellen's dismay, did not know how to conduct himself in such an emergency. Edward did not appear at all. He had said he was very busy, and did not think it was possible he could go, as soon as he heard of Emma's extraordinary request. And though Catherine was almost displeased by his defection, there was nothing to be said against so evident a necessity as that the most active partner in the bank should attend to his work. Her chief point of curiosity in the scene which she surveyed with amused disapproval and astonishment to find herself there, was Hester, to whom her eyes turned with the lively sense of opposition which existed always between the two.

Catherine's eyes, in spite of herself, turned from Emma's insignificance to the fine indignant figure of the girl whom (she said to herself) she could not endure, with the most curious mixture of curiosity, and interest, and rivalship. She, Catherine Vernon, the rival of a trifling creature of nineteen! Such a sentiment sometimes embitters the feelings of a mother towards the girl of whom her son makes choice. But Catherine's mood had nothing to do with Edward. It was more like the "taking sides," which Emma was so anxious to demonstrate was impossible to her as a stranger. Hester had no separate standing ground, no might or authority, and yet it was no exaggeration to say that Catherine, with all of these advantages, instinctively looked upon her as a rival power.

Hester was in the blue dress, which was the alternative of her white one. In those days there were no yellows or sage greens; and even before Catherine remarked the girl's young freshness and beauty, or the high-thrown head, and indignant bearing, which denoted on Hester's side a sense of Catherine's inspection, her eyes had caught the glistening pearls on the young neck—her mother's pearls. Catherine looked at them with a mingled sense of pity and disdain. If that mother had been such a woman as Catherine, neither these pearls nor anything else of value would have remained in her hands. They were Catherine's, they were the creditors' by rights. Mrs. John was not wise enough to understand all that; but Hester, if she knew, would understand. Catherine could not keep her mind from dwelling upon these ornaments. If Hester knew, what would the girl do? Pocket the shame and continue to wear them as became Mrs. John's daughter, or tear them from her neck and trample them under foot? One or the other she would have to do—but then, Hester did not know.

As she walked about through the rooms, stopping to give a gracious word there, a nod here, a question about father or mother, Catherine's mind was not occupied either with the house or the company, but with this girl. Hester had been in the background till now. A glimpse of her in the corner of her own drawing-room, standing by her mother's side in her washed muslin, did not—though Hester's look was always one of indignation—impress her relation's mind. But here she stood like an equal, sending glances of defiance out of her brown eyes. Hester had come in the old fly with the white horse, while Emma was fetched from her grandfather's by Catherine's carriage. The contrast was striking enough; but Catherine, though she would not own it to herself, was more aware than any one else, that no one would look twice at Emma while Hester was by.

When the evening was about half over, Emma came to her patroness and kindly gave her her dismissal.

"Don't wait longer on my account, Cousin Catherine," she said. "I am quite nicely started; thank you so much. I have got my card filled; quite the nicest people in the room have asked me. I'm sure I am very grateful to you, for it is all your doing; but don't think of waiting for me. Chaperons are not at all wanted, and I can go home in Hester's fly. I am so much obliged to you, but of course you want to get to bed. Don't stay a moment longer than you wish, for me."

Catherine smiled, but did not take any further notice. She walked about the rooms for some time after on the arm of Harry, who was always dutiful.

"And who do you think is the prettiest person in the room, Harry? I excuse you from telling me it is my young lady, whom for my own part I don't admire."

"I cannot see there is any doubt about it, Aunt Catherine," said Harry, in his sturdy way. "It is my cousin Hester. There is an air about her—I cannot explain it: I found it out long ago; but now everybody sees it."

"Thanks to her mother's pearls," said Catherine, with her laugh.

Harry looked at her with startled eyes.

"The pearls are very pretty on her; but they are nothing, to me at least," he said.

"You should not let her wear them. She should not have them; knowing her father's story, as I suppose you do.—Don't you see," cried Catherine, with sudden energy, "that she ought not to appear in Redborough in those pearls?"

Emma had been standing near when this conversation began, and she drew closer to listen, not with any clandestine intention, but only with a natural curiosity. She caught up the words in a disjointed way. What reason could there be for not wearing your mother's pearls? She would have gone and asked the question direct of Catherine, but that just then her partner came for her; and for the rest of the evening she had no time to consider any such question; nor was it till she found herself in the fly in the middle of the night rumbling and jolting along the dark road that skirted the Common, by Hester's side, that this mysterious speech occurred to her mind. She had been talking of the advantage of being introduced by a well-known person and thus put at once "on a right footing."

"You don't want that. You know everybody; you have been here all your life," she said. "And I am sure you got plenty of partners, and looked very nice. And what a pretty necklace that is," said Emma, artlessly entering upon her subject. "Are they real? Oh, you must not be offended with me, for I never had any nice ornaments. The youngest never has any chance. If they are real, I suppose they are worth a great deal of money; and you must be quite rich, or you would not be able to afford them."

"We are not rich; indeed we are very poor," said Hester, "but the pearls are my mother's. She got them when she was young, from her mother. They have belonged to us for numbers of years."

"I wonder what Cousin Catherine could mean!" said Emma innocently.

"About my pearls?" cried Hester, pricking up her ears, and all her spirit awakening, though she was so sleepy and tired of the long night.

"She said you oughtn't to wear them. She said you shouldn't have them. I wonder what she meant! And Mr. Harry Vernon, that tall gentleman, he seemed to understand, for he got quite red and angry."

"I oughtn't to wear them—I shouldn't have them!" Hester repeated, in a blaze of wrath. She sat bolt upright, though she had been lying back in her corner indisposed for talk.

"Oh, I dare say she didn't mean anything," said Emma, "only spite, as you are on the other side."

Hester did not reply, but she was roused out of all her sleepiness in a moment. She let Emma prattle on by her side without response. As they drove past the Grange a window was opened softly, and some one seemed to look out.

"Oh, I wonder if that was Mr. Edward," said Emma. "I wonder why he stayed away. Is he after some girl, and doesn't want Cousin Catherine to know? If it were not that you would scarcely speak to each other when you met, I should say it was you, Hester."

"I wish," said Hester severely, "that you would go to sleep; at three in the morning I never want to talk."

"Well, of course, it may be that," said Emma somewhat inconsequently, "but I never want to sleep when I have been enjoying myself. I want to have some one in the same room and to talk it all over—everything that has happened. Who was that man, do you know who——"

And here she went into details which Hester, roused and angry, paid no attention to. But Emma was not dependent on replies. She went on asking questions, of which her companion took no notice, till the fly suddenly stopped with a great jarring and rattling, and the opening of two doors, and glimmers of two small lights in the profound dark, gave note of watchers in the two houses, warned by the slow rumbling of the ancient vehicle, and glad to be released from their respective vigils. In Hester's case it was her mother, wrapped in a warm dressing-gown, with a shawl over her head, and two anxious eyes shining out with warm reflections over her little candle, who received the girl in her finery with eager questions if she were very cold, if she were tired, if all had gone off well.

"Run up stairs, my darling, while I fasten the door," Mrs. John said. "There is a nice fire and you can warm yourself—and some tea."

In those days people, especially women, were not afraid of being kept awake because of a cup of tea.

"Mamma," said Hester when her mother followed her up stairs into the old-fashioned, low-roofed room, which the fire filled with rosy light, "it appears that Catherine Vernon says I ought not to wear your pearls. Has she anything to do with your pearls? Has she any right to interfere?"

"My pearls!" cried Mrs. John almost with a scream. "What could Catherine Vernon have to do with them? I think, dear, you must have fallen asleep and been dreaming. Where have you seen Catherine Vernon, Hester? She gives us our house, dear; you know we are so far indebted to her: but that is the only right she can have to interfere."

"Had she anything to do with my father?" Hester asked.

She was relieved from she did not know what indefinable terrors by the genuine astonishment in her mother's face.

"Anything to do with him? Of course; she had a great deal to do with him. She was his first cousin. Her father had brought him up. It was intended— —but then he met me," said the gentle little woman, not without a tone of satisfaction in the incoherent tale. "And she was a kind of partner, and had a great deal to do with the bank. I never understood the rights of it, Hester. I never had any head for business. Wait, darling, till I undo these buttons. And now, my love, if you have got warm, go to bed. My pearls! She must mean, I suppose, that they are too good for you to wear because we are poor. They were my mother's, and her mother's before that. I would like to know what Catherine Vernon could have to say to them," Mrs. John said, taking the pearls from her child's throat and holding them up, all warm and shining, to the light, before she deposited them in their carefully padded bed.

If there was anything in the world that was her individual property, and in which no one else had any share, it was her pearls: they had always been one of her household gods.

CHAPTER XI
A CENTRE OF LIFE

There are periods in life, and especially in the early part of it, when all existence gets, as it were, out of focus, and instead of some great and worthy centre, takes to circling round some point of outwardly frivolous meaning, some little axis of society entirely unfit to be the turning-point of even the smallest world of human concerns. This had come to be the case with the Vernons in those lingering weeks of winter just before Christmas. That the young, gay, foolish—nay, absurd—house on the hill inhabited by Algernon Merridew and his wife should become to all of this important family the chief place, not only in Redborough, but for a time, in the world, was the most curious fact imaginable; but yet it was so. To Edward it was the one place in the world where he was, as he hoped, free from observation and able to do as he pleased; which meant—where he was entirely free from Catherine, and need have no fear of any interruption from her to his amusement, or his pleasure, or, if you like it better, his love: to Hester it was the place where she had been recognised as part possessor in her own person, like the others, of the honours due to her family, and where the homage, to which a young woman sufficiently endowed has a right, was first given to her; if it had a more close attraction still as the place where she met Edward, that was a dream as yet unacknowledged to her own heart. Harry, on the other hand, had a double interest—neither of them of a very cheerful kind—one of which was the necessity of standing by his sister, who his good sense told him was embarked in a very perilous way, and whose husband was quite incapable of controlling or guiding her erratic course; and the other was the painful fascination of watching Edward and Hester through all the vicissitudes of their quarrellings and makings up—the hours they would spend together, followed by other hours in which they would mutually scowl at each other and did not speak. Harry knew, poor fellow, by a sort of instinct common to the rejected, that the quarrels were as ominous, or more so, than the intimacy. Hester had never quarrelled with himself, they had been on the best terms, alas, as they were now! But Edward she would pass with flushed cheek and shining eye: she would address him with haughty reluctance when it was necessary to speak to him, and mark her reluctance with a decision which was never employed towards those for whom she cared nothing. Harry's eyes were opened, and he understood the duel between them. The only mistake he made was in the belief that it had gone further than the preliminary stage. He could not believe it possible that no explanation had taken place between them.

And of all people to be interested in Ellen's silly parties, who should be seized with an intense desire to know all about them but Catherine Vernon herself? She did know more about them than any one else who was not present, and than a great many who were present. Her suspicions had been roused by various indications of something occult in Edward's mind. He was no longer on his guard to the incredible extent which had been common with him; his mind was agitated with new hopes and fears—the chance of being able to be altogether independent of Catherine had made him relax in his caution, and there had been moments when, in all the stir and elation of his new life, he had been on the eve of disclosing everything. Habitual prudence had saved him, but yet there had been something in his aspect which had roused Catherine's suspicions. They had been, as she thought, in such entire sympathy before, that she was deeply affected by this feeling, which she could not explain to herself—this sense of being in sympathy no longer. And it was all since Ellen's absurd parties began, and he began to meet at them, *that* girl, born for the confusion of all her plans, Catherine thought. There were evenings when the strongest temptation to order her carriage instead of going to bed, and to go suddenly—unexpected—to Ellen's party, and see with her own eyes what was going on, would come over her mind. But there was in Catherine's mind, along with her suspicions, that terror to have them confirmed, which so often goes with love when it begins to tremble in this way. Had she gone, Edward would have declared contemptuously (within himself) that it was all of a piece with her usual watchfulness, and the perfection of her system—not being able to divine that Catherine would have given the world to find herself in the wrong, and shrank from proving herself to be in the right. In the meantime she was kept informed of what was going on more or less by various people, and above all by Emma Ashton, whose information, though largely leavened by a great deal about herself which did not much interest her hearer, also afforded revelations about other people, especially Hester. Emma had become a constant visitor at the Grange. She was allowed to prattle for hours, and Catherine was always kind to her. Her insignificance, her little egotisms, her straightforward aim at her own advancement, did not call forth the amused contempt of that observer of the human comedy as they would have done in any other specimen. Catherine's tradition in favour of her mother's kindred covered this little person with a shield. But those who were not aware of this fond superstition wondered and scorned. And the feeling of the Redborough community was not in Emma's favour.

"She is just a horrid little spy," Ellen cried. "I know she goes and tells Aunt Catherine everything. I shouldn't have her if I could help it; but everybody knows now that she is Aunt Catherine's relation, and they are all civil to her."

"She cannot do us any harm, Nelly," said her husband, "we are not afraid of any spy, I hope."

"Oh, don't talk so much nonsense, Algy," cried Ellen. "Of course she can't do us any harm; but I hate spies for all that."

They were wrong so far that Emma was not at all a spy. Of all the interminable discourses she poured out upon Catherine, the far greater part was about herself; only unfortunately the part that interested her auditor was not that about herself, but the much smaller portion in which, quite unconscious and without any evil motive, she dropped here and there a chance hint as to the others.

"And whom did you say Edward was dancing with?" Catherine would say.

"Oh, I was not talking of Mr. Edward, but of young Mr. Merridew, who is always very attentive. That was our third dance together, and I did feel it was a great pity there were no chaperons, because I should have asked her, if I had been with any one, whether it wasn't rather, you know—for I wouldn't for the world do anything to get myself talked about."

"I thought you had been talking about Edward," Catherine said.

"Oh dear no. It was whether three dances together wasn't perhaps a little—— for I always feel the responsibility of belonging to the family, Cousin Catherine, and I wouldn't for the world do anything——it is quite different with gentlemen. Mr. Edward was just carrying on as usual."

"But, Emma, you must tell me what you mean by 'carrying on.'"

"Oh, I don't mean any harm," Emma would say. "I wonder what young Mr. Merridew is—if he is well off, and all that? Hester has cousins all round to tell her what's best, and of course she does not need to be on her p's and q's, like me."

Catherine had to follow a mazy, vague, and wandering clue thus, through acres of indifferent matter, and to piece together broken scraps of information which were never intended to affect her at all. But they did affect her sometimes so powerfully that she had her hand actually on the bell, not only that evening but on several other occasions, to intimate that she should want the carriage at ten o'clock—a proceeding which would have convulsed the household at home, and carried consternation to the recipients of the unlooked-for honour. But, on further consideration, Catherine always succeeded in subduing herself, often sadly enough saying to herself that it would be time enough when he told her—Why should she go out to meet trouble? Her heart so took her strength from her, and changed her natural temperament, that Catherine restrained herself, with a shrinking, which nobody who knew her would have believed in, from any contact with irresistible fact, and decided that rather than find out the vanity of her confidence it was better to be deceived.

Thus the house on the hill which flaunted forth every Thursday evening the great lamps of its lighted windows and the lines of Chinese lanterns in the conservatory, became the centre for the moment of a great deal of life and many anxious thoughts. It turned Ellen's head with pride and delight when she received indications of this, which indeed came to her on all sides. When a shade of alarm crossed Algernon's face at the amount of the bills, she took a lofty position which no man pretending to any spirit could have gone against. "Goodness, Algy, how can you look so glum about a pound or two, when you see we are doing a great work?" Ellen said. "Well! if it is not more important than mothers' meetings, I don't know what words mean: and Mr. Ransom says the mothers' meetings are a great work." Algernon laughed, but he, too, felt a thrill of pride. To have made the house, which though it was Ellen's was a Merridew house, and his own, into a centre for the great Vernon family, was, if not a great work, at least an extraordinary local success, such as old Merridew's son could never have hoped to attain to. And indeed Algernon's remonstrances about the bills were of the feeblest description. He was too much devoted to his wife to have interfered with her, even had not the balance of moral force been on her side; and he was proud of the extravagance and the commotion and the way in which the elders shook their heads. It is pleasant to make a sensation, and Algernon was comforted by the knowledge that he had already made a little money by his stockbroking transactions, and hoped to make a great deal more.

The young men had carried on their transactions with considerable vigour, though with little risk so far as Algernon and Harry were concerned. But Edward's was a different case. The venture upon which he had pondered with so much anxiety had turned out favourably, and he had gone on without telling his secret to any one, with a general amount of success which had made the operation of risking other people's money seem quite natural to him—a process without any practical consequences at all, except the accumulation of a good deal of money under his own name, which is one of the happiest of sensations. To his temperament indeed it is by no means certain that the vicissitudes of the career in which he had embarked, the tragic suspense in which he was occasionally held, and the transport of deliverance that followed, were not in themselves the highest pleasures of which he was capable. And even so early in his career as this, such crises would come. He had self-command enough not to betray himself when these moments arrived, and though there were eyes keen enough to see that something had produced a change in him, they were, as has been seen in Catherine's case, deceived as to the cause of his perturbation. Hester did not have so many opportunities of studying him, and she had no clue to the business complications in which he was involved; but she had many thoughts on her own mind as to the reason of all the commotion which she saw vaguely, without understanding it. Some of the members of the general society, strangers who sometimes perceive a departure from habit which does not strike the most intimate, had said of Edward on more than one occasion, that he must be in love. Was he in love? Hester had felt that a look was directed to herself when this was said, and that a suppressed laugh had run round the little group. She was herself agitated by tumults which she could not understand, commotions in which Edward was certainly involved, and his name thus mentioned brought the blood to her cheek. Was he in love? She did not want to turn the question upon herself, to bring the matter to any conclusion, one way or another. He was very pale that evening, yet would flush, as she herself did, growing red in a moment and then pale again; and there was a watchful air about him as of a man who expected to hear something or see some one whom nobody else looked for. A man who was in love did not behave so. He was absorbed in the being whom he loved. He is not absorbed in me, the girl said to herself involuntarily, then blushed, as if her thought had been found out. Edward came up to her at this moment, which made her confusion the greater.

"Why do you change colour so? What is the matter?" he said to her.

"It is you who are changing colour," said Hester, not knowing how else to defend herself.

Instead of contradicting her, or throwing off the accusation, he suddenly took her hand and drew it through his arm.

"It is true," he said. "I have something on my mind. You were going to dance this waltz with me. Come into the hall, it is cool there, and let us talk instead?"

Every inch of available space in the house was given up to the accommodation of the guests, and the hall was filled, like the conservatory, with plants, among which little groups of two could find corners. Edward established Hester in one of these, and placed a chair for himself, so as to cut her off from everybody.

"You are the only one that can understand," he said. "I can speak to you. Don't mind me if I look like a fool. I am too anxious to talk."

"What is it?" she said, with a tremour of sympathetic anxiety.

"It is only business," he said, "but it is business so unexpected that even beside you I am obliged to think of it. Can a man say more than that?" he asked with something in his eyes which Hester had never seen there so distinctly before, and which silenced her. One great emotion clears the way for another. Edward in the commotion of his being was almost ready to rush into words that, being said, would have turned his life upside down, and shattered all his present foundations. He was saved by an incident which was of the most ordinary commonplace kind. There came a violent ring at the door which was within half a dozen steps of the spot where they sat. Half a dozen heads immediately protruded from among the little banks of foliage to see what this odd interruption could mean, for all the guests had arrived, and it was not late enough for any one to go away. Hester saw that all the colour ebbed immediately out of Edward's face. He did not even attempt to say a word to her, but sat perfectly still, slightly turned towards the door, but not looking out, awaiting whatever might come. It seemed to Hester that never in her life had she so understood the power of fate, the moment when Nature and life seem to stand still before some event. A minute after, the footman came up and handed a telegram to Edward. He tore it open with trembling hands. The next moment he jumped up from his seat with a suppressed cry of triumph. "Hurrah!" he said, and then with a laugh which was very unsteady held out the despatch to her. All that it contained were the words "All right." But somehow it was not to these words that Hester's eyes confined themselves. "From Ashton, London— —" she said without knowing that she did so, before he thrust the pink paper into his pocket. "Come along," he said, "the waltz is not half over. We shall be in time yet." And for the rest of the evening Edward was in wild spirits, dancing every dance. He even asked the girls to take him with them in their fly as far as the Grange in his reckless exhilaration, and as he got out in the darkness, Hester felt a kiss upon her hand. This startled her still more than the telegram. "Till to-morrow," he said as they rumbled away.

"What does he mean by till to-morrow? He must be coming to make you an offer to-morrow—that is how they do. It often happens after a dance—when it is going to happen," Emma said in the darkness, with a little sigh.

CHAPTER XII
WAS IT LOVE?

Was he in love? That this was a question very interesting to Hester there can be no reason to conceal. She did not even conceal it from herself, nor did she trifle with herself by pretending to suppose that if he were in love it could be with any one else. There was no one else who had ever appeared to attract him. To nobody had he so much as given his passing attention. When he had neglected her at the Grange it had been truly, as he said, for no higher reason than that he might hand down the old ladies to supper or tea. No young one had ever been suggested as having any attraction for him. Hester did her best to enter calmly into this question. It is one which it is sometimes very difficult for a young woman to decide upon. What is conspicuous and apparent to others will often remain to her a question full of doubt and uncertainty; and it is to be feared that when this is the case it is all the more likely that her own sentiments will be capable of very little question. This, however, was not exactly the case with Hester. Her mind was very much interested, and indeed excited. She wanted to know what Edward meant. From the first morning when he had met her, a child wandering on the Common, his manner had been different to her from the manner of other people, or from his own manner to others. His eyes had lingered upon her with pleasure even when his look had been stealthy; even when it had been but a glance in passing, they had said things to her which no other eyes said. His interest in her had never failed. It had not leaped like Harry's, after a good deal of indifference, into a sudden outburst. The very charm and attraction of it had lain in the restraint which Hester had often considered to be dishonest, and against which she had chafed. She had known all through, even in those evenings when he had neglected her, that he was always conscious what she was doing, and knew without looking when any one went to talk to her, when she left the room and when she came back. This had kept her own interest in him unvarying. But Hester was not any more sure of her own sentiments than of his. She remembered with some shame that Roland Ashton's presence had made a great difference in the state of her mind as regarded Edward. She had felt but little curiosity about him when that stranger was at the Vernonry. All the foreground of her mind had been so pleasantly occupied by that new figure which was in itself much more attractive than Edward, that he had slid almost completely out of her thoughts. And this fact, which was only quite apparent to her after Roland was gone, had greatly discomfited Hester, and given her a very small opinion of herself. Was it possible that any new object that might appear would have the same effect upon her? The effect had passed away and Edward had come slowly back to his original position as the person who in all Redborough interested her most. But the incident had been of a very disturbing character, and had altogether confused her ideas. Therefore the question was one of a very special interest. To know exactly how he regarded her would much help her in deciding the other question, not less important, which was, how she regarded him? Everything thus depended, Hester felt, on Edward's sentiments. If it should turn out that he loved her—strange thought which made her heart beat!—it could not be but that in great and tender gratitude for such a gift she should love him. She did feel offended by his efforts to disguise his feelings, or even to get the better of them—never at least when she was cool and in command of her judgment; but there could be no doubt that she was very curious and anxious to know.

Was he in love? The appearances which had made the lookers-on say so were not altogether to be attributed to this, Hester knew. His paleness, his excitement, his absence of mind, had all been from another cause. The discovery had startled her much, and given her an uneasy sense that she might at other times have referred to some cause connected with herself manifestations of feeling which had nothing to do with her, which belonged to an entirely different order of sentiments—a thought which made her blush red with shame, since there is nothing that hurts a girl's pride so much as the suggestion, that she has been vain, and imagined, like the foolish women, a man to love her who perhaps has never thought of her at all. But the question altogether was one which was too profound for Hester. She could not tell what to make of it. Among the heads of the young party at the Merridews, she was aware that no doubt was entertained on the matter. Edward was allotted to her by a sort of unspoken right, and in Ellen's jibes and Harry's gloom she read alike the same distinct understanding. Ellen in her chatter, notwithstanding the warning to her cousin at the beginning, accepted it entirely as a matter of course: and in a hundred things that Edward had said as well as in his looks, which were still more eloquent, there had been strong confirmation of the general belief. But yet—Hester could not make up her mind that it was beyond doubt. She watched him, not with anxiety so much as with a great curiosity. If it was not so, would she be deeply disappointed? she asked herself without being able even to answer that question. And as to her own sentiments, they were quite as perplexing. She was half ashamed to feel that they depended upon his. Was this a confession of feminine inferiority? she sometimes wondered with a hot blush—the position here being very perplexing indeed and profoundly difficult to elucidate; for it neither consisted with the girl's dignity to give her love unsought, nor thus to wait as if ready to deliver up her affections to the first bidder.

Such a matter of thought, involving the greatest interests of life, is curiously mixed up with its most frivolous events. They met in the midst of the dancing with a constant crash and accompaniment of dance-music, amid chatterings and laughter, and all the inane nothings of a ball-room, and yet in the midst of this were to consider and decide the most important question of their lives. It was only thus, except by concerted meetings which would have solved the question, that they could meet at all, and the grotesque incongruity of such surroundings with the matter in the foreground, sometimes affected Hester with a sort of moral sickness and disgust. The scene seemed to throw a certain unworthiness, levity, unelevated aspect upon the question altogether—as if this thing which was to affect two lives was no more than an engagement for a dance.

And though it is a strange thing to say, it is doubtful whether Edward was much more decided in his sentiments than Hester was. In such a case the man at least generally knows more or less what he wants; but partly because Edward's mind was in a high state of excitement on other subjects, he too was for a moment entirely uncertain as to what his wishes were. He knew with sufficient distinctness that he could not tolerate the idea of her appropriation by any one else, and it was his full intention that some time or other Hester should be his, and no one else's, which gave a foundation of certainty to his thoughts which was wanting to hers. But further than this, he too was in a chaos somewhat similar to that of Hester. Sometimes there was in his mind the strongest impulse to tell her that he loved her, and to settle the matter by an engagement, which must, however, he felt, be a secret one, giving satisfaction to themselves but no one else. And here it may be remarked that whereas Hester was apt to be seized by sudden fits of shame at the idea that perhaps, after all her thoughts on the subject, he was not thinking of her at all, Edward on the other hand felt no such alarm, and never thought it even presumptuous on his part to assume the certainty of her love for him, which, as the reader knows, was a certainty to which she had not herself attained. He believed with simplicity that when, if ever (nay, certainly it was to happen some time), he declared himself, Hester would respond at once. He acknowledged to himself that it was possible that in pique, or impatience, or weariness, if he did not keep a vigilant watch over the situation, it might happen that Hester would accept some one else. Her mother might drive her to it, or the impossibility of going on longer might drive her to it; but he had so much confidence in the simplicity of her nature that he did not believe that the complications which held him in on every side could affect her, and was sure that in her heart the question was solved in the most primitive way.

This was and generally is the great difference between the man and woman in such a controversy; until he had spoken, it was a shame to her that she should ask herself did he intend to speak; but Edward felt no shame if ever the idea crossed his mind that he might be mistaken in supposing she loved him; such a discovery would have made him furious. He would have aimed all sorts of ill names, such as coquette and jilt, at her; but he had no fear of any such mistake. He felt sure that he had her in his power, and when he did declare himself would be received with enthusiasm; and he always meant to declare himself some time, to reward her long suspense, and to make her the happiest of women. In words, this part is generally allotted to the lady, as it was in the days of chivalry. But the nineteenth century has modified many things, and if ever (out of America) it was really the woman who occupied the more commanding position, it is no longer so in the apprehension of the world. Only in this particular case, as has been seen, Edward was wrong. It is possible enough that in the curious position of affairs between them she would have followed his lead whatever it might be; but even this was by no means certain, and as a matter of fact, though her curiosity about him drew her mind after him, she had not even gone so far as he had, nor come to any ultimate certainty on the case at all.

Emma Ashton, who by means of propinquity—that quick knitter of bonds—had become Hester's frequent companion, had very different ideas on a similar subject. There was no sort of indefiniteness in her views. She was perfectly clear as to what she was likely to do in a given case, and the case in question occupied probably almost as great a share in her thoughts as the different yet similar question which agitated the mind of Hester. It was indeed to outward view, though with so many and subtle differences, a very similar question. Emma's wonder was whether Reginald Merridew would "speak" before she went away. She had no doubt that all the requisite sentiments were existing, and she had satisfied herself that when he did "speak" there was no reason why she should not reply favourably. The family was "quite respectable," it might almost be said also that it was "quite well off," but that there were rumours that Algernon was to be "made an eldest son of," which were somewhat disquieting. The suggestion was one which made Emma indignant, notwithstanding the gratitude she owed Algernon and his wife for giving her "her chance" in Redborough.

"When there is an estate I suppose it is all right," Emma said; "anyhow it can't be helped when that's the case; and there must be an eldest son. But when your property is in money it does seem such a mistake to make a difference between your children. Don't you think so? Oh, but I do; they are just one as good as another, and why should one be rich and another poor? If old Mr. Merridew does anything of this sort I am sure I shall always think it is very unfair."

"I suppose Mr. Merridew has a right to do what he pleases?" said Hester; "and as it does not matter to us— —"

"You speak a great deal too fast," said Emma, offended. "Say it doesn't matter to you: but it may to me a great deal, and therefore I take a great interest in it. Do you think parents have a right to do what they please? If they make us come into the world, whether we wish it or not, of course they are bound to do their best for us. I am the youngest myself, and I hope I know my place; but then there was no money at all among us. Papa spent it all himself; so certainly we had share and share alike, for there was nothing. When that's the case nobody can have a word to say. But the Merridews have a good deal, and every one ought to have his just share. Not but what I like Algernon Merridew very much. He is always very agreeable, and I think it very nice both of Ellen and him that they should have been so kind to me and given me my chance, though you say we're no relations. I am sure I always thought we were relations, for my part."

"Did you think Reginald was your relation too?"

"Well, not perhaps quite so far as that—a connection I should have said; but it does not matter very much now," Emma said, with a little simper of satisfaction. "What a good thing Roland found out about grandpapa and grandmamma, Hester—and how fortunate that they should have asked *me*! If everything goes right I shall feel that I owe the happiness of my life to it. When a girl goes out upon a visit, she never knows what may happen before she gets home—or even she may never need to go home at all. I don't know if I shall, I am sure. To talk about anything taking place from Roland's house would be absurd. Why, we don't even know the clergyman! and nobody cares a bit about us. If there was any meaning in home it should be from Elinor's, you know—for everybody knows us there."

"What do you mean about 'anything taking place'?—and from—from what?" Hester asked, who never paid too much attention to Emma's monologues, and had altogether lost the thread of her discoursings now.

"Oh," cried Emma, clasping Hester's arm close, "how you do make one blush! Of course you know very well what I mean. If he speaks before I go away—and I am sure I hope he will, for it would be such a nuisance to have him following me up to Kilburn!—I don't suppose there would be any occasion for waiting long. Why should people wait when they are well off enough, and nothing to be gained by it? When the man has not got settled in a proper situation, or when there is not enough to live upon, then of course they must put it off; but in such a case as ours—I mean this, you know—it might as well be here as anywhere," Emma said, reflectively. "Cousin Catherine has always been very kind to me. Rather than let grandpapa and grandmamma be disturbed at their age, I shouldn't wonder if she would give the breakfast—especially considering the double connection, and that it is such a very good thing to get me settled. You needn't laugh, Hester. It is not a thing to laugh at. Unless I had settled, what should I have done? You are an only daughter, you don't know what it is to be the youngest and have no proper home."

These words mollified Hester, who had been in lofty opposition, half disgusted, half indignant. She was brought down by this appeal to her sympathy. "But you are happy with your brother?" she said.

"Oh, yes—happy enough; Roland is very kind. And though it's a small house, it is tolerably nice, and two maids with nothing particular to do. But it is very dull, you know, and I don't know many people. And you must always take into consideration that at any moment Roland might marry, and then where should I be? Why, he admires you very much. He might just as likely as not, next time he comes, make you an offer; and then where should I be?"

"You think, I suppose," said Hester, loftily, "that when a man makes an offer, as you say, that is all about it; there is no opposition to be looked for on the girl's side?"

"Well, you know," said Emma, "I call you one of the high-flown ones. There are always some like that. But in an ordinary way what do girls want but their chance? And when they've got it, what folly to refuse—at least in my position, Hester. If I don't get settled, what have I to look forward to? Roland will marry sooner or later. He's an awful flirt, and though he admires you very much, I shouldn't advise you to have anything to do with him unless you just marry him out and out. I should think he'd make a good husband. But don't be engaged to him, Hester; mind my words. Be married in three weeks, or have nothing to say to him—that is my advice. Oh, you need not be huffy. I am sure I don't want you or any one to marry him, at least till I am settled. But if I don't settle now, he is sure, of course, to marry some time; and then where shall I be? This is what makes me wish that if—*he*, you know, is going to speak, he would do it, and not shilly-shally. It is astonishing how men shilly-shally. I think they take a pleasure in it. They would know better if they had to wait as we have, and wonder, and feel that we can't make any arrangements or settle anything till we know what's coming. If I have to go away and he never says anything, I don't know what I shall do."

"Is this because you—care so much for Reginald Merridew?" Hester could not so form her lips as to say love.

Emma made a sort of reflective pause. "I like him well enough," she said. "I am not one to go on about love and so forth. Besides, that sort of thing is not becoming in a girl. You can't, till you are quite certain what *they* mean, don't you know? It is dreadful to go caring for them, and all that, and then to find out that they don't care for you. A girl has to wait till they speak."

Hester listened not with her usual mixture of amusement and indignation, but with a curious feeling of shame and alarm growing in her. Was not this what she herself was doing? Emma's desire that her supposed lover should speak and settle the question, was it not much the same thing as her own curiosity and self-questioning in respect to Edward? Emma was always more practical. She was so in sentimental matters as well as in everything else. Things that other people leave indistinct, in a half light, she put clearly, without any pretences at obscurity. Her grieved sense of the shilly-shallying of men, her consciousness of all the inconveniences that arose from their way of putting off their explanations, her prudential conviction that a girl should not commit herself by "caring for" *them*, before they made it apparent that they cared for her—were these not so many vulgar, straightforward statements of the dilemma in which Hester too found herself? But this grotesque resemblance of sentiment and situation made Hester, as may be supposed, passionately angry and indignant, not with Emma, who was guiltless, and who pursued the subject endlessly, never tiring of it, nor of going over the matter again and again from the beginning as they walked, but with herself and Edward, and fate, which had placed her in such circumstances. It was something like a caricature of herself that was thus presented to her, and she could scarcely help laughing at it, even while she resented it warmly as an insult offered to her by—whom? not Emma—by circumstances and evil fortune, and the spite of a position which was intolerable, and Catherine Vernon. All these persons were conspiring against her, but none of them were so hard upon Hester as this little purring deliberate Emma, holding up her little distorted mirror that Hester in her pride might see how like was the image in it to her own troubled face.

CHAPTER XIII
CHRISTMAS

While all these agitations were going on, it came to be Christmas, with the usual stir and commotion always produced in a large family and connections, by that often troublesome festival. The amount of reality in the rejoicings may be very doubtful, but yet there must be a family gathering, and the different branches of the race must seem to take kindly to it whatever may be their private sentiments. Dickens did wisely in finding his types of Christmas felicity among people to whom an accidental turkey is a benediction from heaven, and the mystery of the pudding has not lost its freshness. In such a family as the Vernons, the turkey and the pudding are unsatisfactory symbols—a return to the rude elements of plenty which were employed by a more primitive age; and though it certainly was an excitement for the Miss Vernon-Ridgways, and Mr. Mildmay Vernon and Mrs. John, to be invited to dinner, it was by no means invariable that their feast improved the harmony of these much separated divisions of the family. It was a very big dinner, and there was no absolute breach of the peace. Catherine sat at the head of the table in a dress which, though very handsome, was by no means one of her best, and without the diamonds in which she appeared on very great occasions. This was kindly intended, in order that she might not make too evident the contrast between her own toilette and that of some of her visitors; but the kindness of the intention was not appreciated.

"We are not considered worth dressing for," Miss Matilda said, in her sister's ear, after they had respectively kissed their relative, and, with effusion, wished her a merry Christmas.

"She thinks it better taste to be as shabby as we are," said the other, which indeed was very true, though no offence was meant.

As for Mrs. John, though she was quite willing to enjoy herself, her mind was kept in a state of nervous anxiety about Hester, who was in the defiant mood with which she always met her cousin. It had been her mother's desire to dress her plainly in one of the simple dresses made up on the foundation of the "silk slip," which by this time had been worn out as a ball-dress. These economies were very necessary, and indeed it ought to be said that the ball-dresses could not have been kept up as they were, but for the sacrifice of Mrs. John's Indian shawl, which, after Hester and the pearls, was the thing in the world which the poor lady held most dear.

Hester had not resisted the substitution of the simpler dress for those carefully preserved clouds of tarlatan which were sacred to the Dancing Teas. But she stood firm to the pearls, and insisted on wearing them. "Unless you will put them on yourself, mamma," she said.

"I wear them, Hester! Oh, no! They have been in their box all these years, and I have never put them on, you know. I kept them for you. But don't you think, dear, that just for a family dinner—no one is expected to be fine at a family dinner——"

"Don't you want Catherine Vernon to see them, mother? If it is so, tell me at once."

"Don't I want Catherine Vernon—to see them?" cried Mrs. John, stupefied with astonishment. "I wonder," she added, regretfully, "what there is between you that makes you lose your good sense, Hester—for you are very sensible in most things, and far cleverer than I ever was—the moment Catherine Vernon's name is mentioned? I cannot think what it can be."

"Oh, mother! You are too good—if that is what not being clever means. When I think how you have been allowed to stand in the corner of that room, and nobody taking any notice of you."

"My dear," said Mrs. John, mildly, "I did not require to go unless I liked."

"And now this dinner—a sort of Christmas dole for her relations—like the flannel petticoats to the poor women."

"We do not require to go unless we like," said Mrs. John; "but if you will reflect a little, Hester, that is not how a lady should talk."

It was seldom that the mild little woman said so much. When Hester came up to Catherine, following her mother's little figure, clothed in a black silk gown which had seen a great deal of service, she read, with an excitement that made her glow, that Catherine's first glance was upon the pearls.

"You are quite fine," she said as she went through the Christmas formula, and dropped a formal kiss upon Hester's reluctant cheek; "you have put on your lovely pearls to do us honour."

"She is fond of the pearls," said Mrs. John, who was very watchful to prevent any collision; "they were her grandmother's, and her great-grandmother's, Catherine. It is not only for their value that one is fond of things like these."

"Their value is sometimes the worst thing about them," said Catherine, feeling that there was a sternness of virtue in what she said which justified her dislike. But Mrs. John stood her ground.

"I don't think so," she said simply. "I like them to be worth a great deal, for they are all she will have."

Hester, thus talked over, stood drawing back, in all her flush of youthful indignation, kept down by the necessities of the occasion. She gave a glance round at the little audience which was enjoying the encounter, the Miss Vernon-Ridgways in the foreground. She caught their keen inquisitive stare, and the mantling of delight upon their faces as they witnessed the little passage of arms; and Mr. Vernon Mildmay craning over their shoulders with his sharp face projected to see what it was, and Mrs. Reginald's countenance half sympathetic, half-preoccupied (for to-day for the first time her eldest boy had accompanied her, and she was very anxious lest he should do or say anything that might injure him with Catherine). But the one thing Hester did not catch was Edward's eyes, which surely, if he had cared for her, ought now to have been raised in kindness. He was outside of the circle, his head turned away, taking no notice. When Mrs. John fell back to give way to Ellen Merridew, who came up rustling and jingling with all her bracelets, Edward still kept apart. He was talking to Harry, to Algernon, to everybody except the two who, Hester felt, wanted the succour of a chivalrous sympathy. But Mrs. John had no feeling of this kind. She felt that she had held her own. She looked with a mild pride upon the group of her neighbours all so eagerly watching for mischief. It was natural, when you think of it, that she should treat the ill-nature of the Miss Vernon-Ridgways with gentle disdain. Poor things! they had neither a daughter nor a necklace of pearls. And as she had not been at the *Thés dansantes*, nor seen Edward in any aspect but that he had always borne at the Grange, she felt no anxiety as to his present behaviour. Harry's was the eye which she sought. She beamed with smiles when he came and stood beside her. Harry was always faithful, whoever might be careless. She looked at him and at Hester with a little sigh; but who could tell what might happen with patience and time?

There was, however, one moment during the evening in which Edward had the opportunity of setting himself right. It was while the departures were going on, while the ladies were being shawled and cloaked. Catherine had not come down stairs, and in the darkness of the further corner of the hall, under cover of the chatter of Ellen and Emma Ashton, the young man ventured upon a hurried whisper—

"Do you despise me or detest me most?" he said in Hester's ear. She started—what with the sudden proximity, what with the unexpected character of the question.

"I wonder?" she answered coldly. He took the opportunity of wrapping her cloak round her to grasp both her hands in a sudden, almost fierce grasp.

"You could do nothing less: but I cannot be different here. Suspicion produces treachery, don't you know?" he said, with his face close to her ear. "I cannot be true here. No, don't say anything. I ought, but I cannot. It is in the air. All of us, every one except you, we are making believe and finding each other out, yet going on all the same. But it is only for a time," Edward cried, grasping her hands once more till the pressure was painful, "only for a time!"

Next moment he was standing at the door, impassible, saying good-night to every one, paying no more heed to Hester than if she had been, as indeed she was, the least important of all the Christmas visitors. Ellen, as a married woman and a social power, commanded his attention, and to Emma, as the stranger among so many who knew each other, he was very polite. But Hester got from him the coolest good-night. The very servants who stood about, felt a passing wonder that the prettiest person in the company should meet with such scant observation, but explained it by saying to each other that "Mr. Edward, he was the one as kep' hold of the main chance."

And Hester went home, angry, yet somewhat soothed. It did not make her less indignant, less wrathful; but it gave an excuse which at least had to be taken into consideration. Before she got home, indeed, she taught herself to lay that offence too to the score of Catherine. She went home packed into the fly with her mother and Emma and the Miss Vernon-Ridgways, all together. Mr. Mildmay Vernon was mounted on the box, and the old white horse had the six people, besides his driver, to drag behind him. He took a great deal of time over the short bit of road, thinking probably that it was as well to take his time over one fare as to put it in the power of his oppressors to send him out with another, or perhaps compel him to kick his heels at the railway station waiting for the last train. The ladies were packed very close inside, but not too close to talk. The sisters immediately plunged into that "criticism of life" which could scarcely be called poetry, in their hands.

"What a blessing it is," said one, "that we can't be called upon to eat another Christmas dinner with Catherine for another year."

"Dear Catherine!" said the other, "she always means so well. It is our own fault if we don't carry out her intentions."

"Indeed," said Mrs. John, "she gave us a very nice dinner, and everything was very comfortable."

"Dear Mrs. John! you are always so charitable," said Miss Matilda, "as we all ought to be, I am sure. Did you ever see anything so insufferable as that little Ellen—like a picture out of a fashion-book—giving herself as many airs as if she were at the head of society? I never heard she had any society, except the vulgar young people on the Thursdays. I wonder she doesn't ask her shop people."

"Oh, hush, hush!" cried Mrs. John, alarmed.

"Perhaps she does ask the shop people," said Miss Matilda, "it would be wise of her, for I should not think they'd ever see the colour of their money. The old Merridews can never keep up all that extravagance, and Algy is nothing more than a clerk in his father's office. It is dreadful to see a young man dragged on to destruction like that."

"Oh, I hope it is not so bad!" cried Mrs. John. "I am sure if I thought so, I should never let— —"

"It is the talk of the town," said Miss Matilda. "A thing must be very bad before it comes to us, who never hear any gossip."

"Oh, everybody knows," said Miss Martha.

It was happy that Hester's mind was so fully occupied, and that the conversation passed harmlessly over her head. When they reached the Vernonry, Mr. Mildmay Vernon got down from the box where he had been seated wrapped up from head to foot, but which he protested against with a continuous volley of short coughs as he helped the ladies out one after another. He thought in his heart that if one of these strong young women had been put up on the box, who had no rheumatism, it would have been more appropriate.

"I hope you have enjoyed your evening, including your dinner," he said. "I have made up my mind to rheumatism to-morrow; but what does that matter in comparison with such a delightful entertainment?"

"It was very nice," said Mrs. John, dubious as to his meaning, as she always was.

"Nice!" he said, with a grimace, "a sort of little heaven on earth!"

"It is wicked to be so satirical," said one sister, with a laugh; and "Dear Catherine! I am sure she meant everything that was kind," said the other.

And then there was a little flutter of good-nights, the respective doors opening, and lights flashing out into the dark.

This entertainment was followed very shortly after by the larger gathering which Catherine had announced her intention of giving some time before, and to which all Redborough was convoked besides the immediate family. The period between these two parties was the climax of Hester's hostility to Catherine Vernon. She had never been so actively indignant, so angry, nor so impotent against her old and wealthy cousin as in these wintry days. Catherine was a kind of impersonation of injustice and unkindness to

Hester. She felt not only that she herself was oppressed and injured, but that the persecution of which she was the object was of a kind which was most petty and miserable, degrading to the author of it as well as to its victim. The attempt at interference with her movements was not only a kind of meddling most irritating to a high-spirited girl, but it was also the kind of assault which her very pride prevented her from resisting openly. Hester felt that she would have lowered her own pride, and wounded her own self-respect, had she uttered a word of reply or taken any notice of the small and petty attack upon her. The incident of the pearls, though so trifling, excited her almost as much as the other and more important grievance she had against Catherine. That Edward should be so cowed by this woman that he had to conceal his real sentiments, to offend the girl whom he loved, to compromise his own honour and dignity all because of Catherine's watch upon him, and the subjection in which it held him, was such a miserable thought to Hester, that it was all she could do to restrain herself at all. It is terrible to be compelled to endure one who has harmed those who are dear to you; but to enter her house and preserve a show of peace and good-feeling, though you are aware she is causing the self-debasement of those you love, that is the hardest of all. What should it matter to Edward that Catherine's eye was upon him? An honourable and fine spirit would not have been influenced by any such oppression. It made Hester's heart sick to think that he did this consciously, deceived his benefactress, and pretended to obey her when in his heart he loathed his bondage; and to think that she herself should be called upon to sustain this humiliation filled her with shame and rage. But though her heart was bitter against Edward, there was yet a softening in it, an involuntary indulgence, which made her glad to elude the question so far as he was concerned, and to fix upon Catherine, who was the cause of it, with all her force of indignation.

From Hester's point of view there was indeed little to be said for this woman, who, to so many in the place, was the very impersonation of active benevolence and goodness—a tyrant who seized upon the very soul of the young man whom she favoured most, and whose prying and vigilant observation forced him to deception, and made him true to himself only when he was out of her sight—a woman, who while she gave with one hand closed a grasp of iron upon the people obliged to her with the other, and would prescribe their very dress if she could. Oh, how true it must be after all, the picture of the tyrannical, narrow despot, exacting, remorseless, descending to the lowest details, which a woman, when endued with irresponsible power, was understood to make! Hester had rebelled as a girl does against every such injurious picture of women; but it occurred to her now that it must all be true. No doubt it was unsafe to trust such a creature with any kind of authority. She would not be content with less than absolute sway. She would let no charity nor ruth, nor the hearts of others, nor their wishes, stand in her way. She would crush a young life with no more compunction than a savage. Thus Hester took refuge from questions more trying—from the aspect of Edward which within these last few days had become more and more important to her. Her whole being seemed to be flowing towards him with a current which she felt herself unable to restrain. She did not any longer ask herself questions about his love. She tried not to ask any questions about him at all. In her secret consciousness there was a distrust of him, and disapproval and fear, which had never been breathed into any ear—scarcely even into her own. Indeed, Hester was her own only confidant. All the things which occupied her were uncommunicable. She had grown a woman, everything that happened was now more important to her than in earlier days. And now there had come a crisis in her fate, and it was not she who held the key of the problem, nor her lover, nor any legitimate authority—but Catherine! Catherine controlled her future and all its issues through him. Catherine could have stopped all further development for both, she could have checked their love ruthlessly, and made an end of their happiness. The girl began to feel that there was something in the presence of this woman, in her influence, in her very name, that was insupportable. That impulse of flight which always presents itself to the impatient spirit came upon her strongly. Why should not she and her mother shake themselves free from the imbroglio—go away anywhere, it did not matter where, and get peace, at least, and a life free of agitations and complications? Away from the Vernons she would be free to work as she pleased, and so make up for the aid that Catherine gave—away from them there would be no more question of love and hate, love afraid to declare itself, hate veiled beneath the aspect of benevolence.

Hester had very little to do at home. She had not even books to read. She had unbounded time to think; even her visits to her old friends, the captain and his wife, had grown less frequent since Emma came, for Emma's monologues were not amusing to Hester's excited mind, and the captain and Mrs. Morgan had both yielded to their granddaughter's irrepressible talent of speech. Hester was more at home in consequence, more alone, less subject to wholesome distractions and interruptions. She would think and think the whole evening through. The *Thés dansantes* began to fill her with a sort of sickening, of weariness, and disgust. She felt as if she too, like Emma, had gone to get her "chance" there, and was, like Emma, hung up in degrading suspense until he should speak. The rage with her position, the scorn of herself with which this filled her, is indescribable. She would burst forth into wild laughter after one of Emma's calculations, often repeated, about Reginald Merridew; then hide her face in her hands to conceal the burning blush—the bitter consciousness that her own circumstances were not much different. The self-ridicule was more painful still than the self-disgust. She shed no tears over the question, but the laughter was a great deal more bitter than any tears.

Mrs. John was as unconscious of this struggle as if it had gone on in Kamschatka and not under her own eye, in her own parlour, and the bedroom that opened into hers. She was not one of the women who divine. She understood what was told her, and not always that—never anything more than was told her. She thought her child was not looking well, but then, she had a cold; and there is nothing more oppressive than a cold. The first thing that really startled her was Hester's determination not to go to Mrs. Merridew's party on the first Thursday that occurred after Christmas, which was to be a particularly brilliant one. This struck her mother with consternation.

"Do you think your cold is so bad as that? I would not wish you to do anything imprudent, but I have often heard girls say that a ball was the very best thing for a cold. If you were to nurse up this evening, and have your breakfast in bed, I can't help thinking you would feel quite yourself to-morrow, my darling," Mrs. John said.

"It is not my cold," said Hester; and then she reflected that it was a pity to throw aside so excellent a plea. "At least it is not altogether my cold."

"Oh, I know how oppressed one feels, just good for nothing; but, my love, you would feel sorry after. It is a pity to give in. You shall have a foot-bath to-night with some mustard in it, and a hot drink. And you must not get up till mid-day. You'll feel a great deal better after that."

"I don't want to go—I am tired of them," Hester said, her impatience getting the better of her, "once a week is a great deal too often. I am sick of the very name of dancing."

"My love!" cried her mother in consternation. Then she came behind her and gave her a soft little kiss. "I think I shall give you quinine, for I am sure you're low," she said, "and you must be bright and well, and looking your best for Catherine's great party, which is next week."

"I don't——" cried Hester, then stopped short, for she had not the heart to give her mother a double wound by declaring she would not go to Catherine's party. One such blow was enough at a time.

The astonishment with which her non-appearance at Mrs. Merridew's was regarded by all the connection was unbounded. The discovery that Hester *was not going*, filled the Miss Ridgways with excitement. What could be the cause?

"I suppose there has been a quarrel," the sisters said. "Ellen is a little minx; but still she is a true Vernon, and won't stand any such airs as that girl gives herself. Her mother and she are insupportable, with their pearls and their pretences."

"Roman pearls," said Mr. Mildmay Vernon, "and Brummagem pretences."

So they discussed the question. When Hester went in next day to Captain Morgan's, not without a little curiosity to hear from Emma what had been said of her absence: "I am glad you have recovered," Mrs. Morgan said, kissing her, and looking into her face with an air of reproach and a shake of the head.

"It is not like you to give in for a cold," the old captain added; but fortunately for Hester all explanation on her part, and all remonstrance on theirs, was cut short by the persevering deliberate voice which now was the principal circumstance in the old people's house.

"I assure you Ellen was very much astonished, Hester. She looked at me as if she could not believe her eyes. And they all looked at me as if it was my fault. How could it be my fault? I didn't give you your cold. I think there were more people than usual. We had Sir Roger de Coverley, you know, because it was Christmas. I danced it with young Mr. Norris, who has just come into his fortune, you know. He is very nice. He asked me for four dances, but I only gave him three. Don't you think I was right, grandmamma? That is the worst of Ellen's parties, that there are no old chaperons with experience, that could advise you on a point like that. Two waltzes and then the Sir Roger, which is a sort of extra you know, and doesn't count. I don't think there could be anything wrong in that."

"You should not give in, Hester," said the old captain. "That is not like you. What is a cold at your age! You should always stand to your colours, and hold your— —"

"Oh, I said to everybody, Hester had such a bad cold," said Emma. "I said that her nose was red and that it quite affected her voice. So it does. You don't notice it so much when she flames up like that. I wonder how you can blush in that way, Hester. It is the difference of complexion, I suppose. I always keep the same. It is nice in some ways, for however hot it is you can be sure you are not a figure; but in other respects I should like to change colour like that. It makes you look interesting. People think you are so sensitive, and that sort of thing, when it's only just complexion. Harry Vernon was more grumphy than ever because you were not there, always standing about beside Ellen and looking after her, which, considering she's married, is a great deal more than any brother ought to take upon him. I am sure if Roland did, I should not know what to think. But then Ellen is an only sister, which makes a great difference, and I am the youngest. Reginald Merridew was in such a way! I was engaged for almost every dance before he came. I quite enjoyed it. I filled up my card as soon as I could, just to give him a lesson. Men should be kept in their proper places. I never thought you showed half a spirit letting Edward Vernon carry you off just as he pleased."

"My dear," said old Mrs. Morgan, making an endeavour to strike in, we have not seen half so much of you lately as we like to do. My old man misses you on his walk. Do go and take a walk with him, as your cold is better."

"Oh, don't send her away when I just want to talk over everything," said Emma. "You never think what young people like. I am sure you are very kind and nice, grandmamma, I always say so. Whatever any one may think, I always maintain that you have been very nice and kind to me: and kept me such a time—when I dare say you are tired of me. But you don't remember what young people like. Of course Hester wants to hear who was there, and how every one was looking, and who danced with who, and all that. There are always a hundred things that we have to say to each other. Come up with me to my room, Hester, and then we sha'n't bore grandmamma and grandpapa. I have such a lot to tell you. Ellen had such a lovely new dress, old gold and black. It sounds much too old for her, but it wasn't a bit. It was quite a change among all the whites and pinks. I just went in my grenadine. I don't pretend to cope with the rich girls, you know. If the men want to dance with rich dresses they must just leave me alone. I am always straightforward. I say, 'Don't ask me unless you are sure you don't mind.' But I suppose they like my dancing or something, for I always have my card full. Sir Roger de Coverley was really fun. We were all dancing, it seemed about a mile going down the middle. It is such a pity you weren't there. Edward Vernon danced it with—I really forget who he danced it with—one of the Miss Bradleys or Mary Wargrave, or one of that set. Are you really going out with grandpapa? That is awfully self-denying of you, to please the old gentleman. And it is so cold. Grandmamma, I do think you shouldn't let her go."

"She can hear your report another time—indeed she has heard a great deal of it already," said old Mrs. Morgan. "You don't lose any time, Emma. But, Hester, if you are afraid——"

"Oh, I shouldn't go on any account," cried Emma, "with a bad cold. But then I have such dreadful colds when I do have them. I am obliged to go to bed. I never get my nose red like Hester's, nor lose my voice—but I get such a cough. I am so thankful I have not had one here. It gives everybody so much trouble when you get ill on a visit, and you lose all the good of the visit, and might just as well be at home. There is grandpapa calling. I should just let him call if it was me. Well, Hester, if you will go, I can't help it. Come in again if you are not afraid of the evening air, and you shall hear all the rest; or if you'll have me at tea time, perhaps that will be best. I'll go to you——"

The old captain sighed as he went out. Emma was, as it were, left speaking, standing on the step of the door addressing Hester, as she followed her old friend out into the dusky afternoon of one of those black days that conclude the year. Very black days they were on this occasion, not so cold as December often is, without snow or any of the harsher signs of winter, but also without sun or any of the exhilarating sharpness of the frost. Everything was dry, but dark, the skies leaden, the very Common showing less green. The captain went on before with a woollen comforter wrapped in many folds about his throat, and woollen mittens on the hands which grasped his stick with so much energy. He struck it against the ground as if he had been striking some one as he hurried away.

"I think that girl will be the death of us," he said: then repented of his sharp utterance. "I told you I thought you were a spiritual grandchild, Hester. What the child of our child whom we lost, who never had a child, would have been. And you have spoiled us for the other thing—the grandchild of common life."

"It is a long time since we have been out together," said Hester, as the old man put his other hand in its large mitten within her slender arm.

"And you have been in the meantime getting into some of the muddles," he said. "It was kind of my old wife to hand you over to me, Hester. We all think our own experience the best. She would like to have had you to herself, to find out all about it, and give you the help of her old lights; but instead of that she was self-denying, and handed you over to me. And now let me hear what it is, and see if the old ship's lantern will do you any good."

"Am I in any muddles?" said Hester. "I don't know—perhaps there is nothing to tell. It is so hard to divide one thing from another."

"So it is; but when it is divided it is easier to manage," said the old captain. He paused a little to give her time to speak: but as she did not do so he resumed on an indifferent subject, that the girl's confidence might not be forced. "I am always glad when the old year is over. You will say I am an old fool for that, as my days are so few. But the first of January is a great deal gayer than the first of December, though they may be exactly like each other. When you can say there will be spring this year— —"

"Captain Morgan," said Hester, who had been taking advantage of the pause without paying any attention to what he said, "Catherine Vernon is angry because I wear my mother's pearls. How should that be?"

"You must be mistaken, my dear," said the old captain promptly. "She has her faults, but Catherine is never paltry, Hester. That cannot be."

"Either you are very much mistaken about her, or I am much mistaken about her," Hester said.

The old man looked at her with a smile on his face.

"I don't say anything against that. And which of us is most likely to be right?" he asked. "I knew her before you were born."

"Oh, before I was born! Does that tell you anything about her conduct to *me*? Once I was not, but now I am; and somebody quite distinct from other people."

"Very distinct!" Captain Morgan said.

"Then what does she mean by it?" cried Hester. "She cannot endure the sight of me. Oh, I know she is not paltry in one way. She does not care about money, as some people do; but she is in another. Why should she care about what I wear? Did you ever hear anything about my father?" the girl said, raising her eyes suddenly, and looking him full in the face. The old captain was so taken by surprise that he fell back a step and almost dropped her arm in his dismay.

"About your father!"

"About him and Catherine Vernon—and how it was he went away? He had as good a right to the bank as she had, had he not? I have not thought much about it; but I should like to know," said Hester with more composure, "how it was that she had it and not papa?"

"That was all before my time," said Captain Morgan, who had recovered himself in the interval. "I did not come here, you know, till after. And then it is not as if I had been a Vernon to understand all the circumstances. I was not of the family, you know."

"That is true," said Hester thoughtfully, and she suffered herself to be led into safer subjects without any serious attempt to return to a question so unanswerable; while Captain Morgan on his side was too much alarmed by the possibility of having to explain to her the steps which had led to her father's expatriation to inquire any more into the "muddles" which he had read in her countenance. And thus they made their way home together without any mutual satisfaction. The captain was obliged to own to his wife afterwards that he had given Hester no aid or good advice.

"She asked me about her father: and was I going to be so brutal as to tell the poor child what has always been concealed from her?"

"Concealments are never good," Mrs. Morgan said, shaking her head. "It would be better for her to know." But the captain had an easy victory when he said "Should you like to be the one to tell her?" with defiance in his voice.

Thus the time went on for Catherine Vernon's great Christmas party, to which all Redborough was asked. It was not till the day before that Hester was bold enough to declare her intention not to go. "You must not be angry, mamma. What should I go for? It is no pleasure. The moment I am in Catherine Vernon's house I am all wrong. I feel like a beggar, a poor relation, a dependent upon her charity; and she has no charity for me. Don't make me go."

"Oh Hester, my darling," said Mrs. John. "It would never, never do to stay away, when everybody is there! And you her relation, that ought to wish to do her what honour you can."

"Why should I wish to do her honour? She has never been kind to us. She has never treated you as she ought to have done. She has never behaved to us as a relation should, or even as a gentlewoman should."

"Oh hush! Hester, hush!" said Mrs. John. "You don't know what you are speaking of. If you knew all, you would know that Catherine has behaved to us—better than we had any right to expect."

"Then let me know all, mother," said Hester, sitting upright, her eyes shining, her whole face full of inquiry. "I have felt lately that there must be something which was concealed from me. Let me know all."

Then Mrs. John faltered and explained. "There is nothing for you to know. Dear, dear, you are so literal. You take everything one says to you, Hester, as if one meant it. There are just things that one says— —When I said if you knew all, I meant—if you were to consider properly, if you saw things in a just light— —"

"I think you mean something more than that," Hester said.

"What should I mean more? We had no claims upon her. Your poor father had got his share. He had not perhaps been very prudent with it, but I never understand anything about business. He got his share, all that he had any right to expect. Catherine might have said that, when we came back so poor; but she did not. Hester, you have forgotten what she has done for us. Oh, my dear, if you knew all! No, I don't mean that there is anything to know—but just if you would think—Hester, you must not insult Catherine in the sight of all Redborough by refusing to go to her party. You must not, indeed you must not. If you do, you will break my heart."

"What I do is of no importance to Catherine Vernon. Oh, mother, do not make me go. It is more than I can bear."

"But you are of importance, and she would feel it deeply. Oh, Hester, for my sake!" Mrs. John cried with tears in her eyes. She would not be turned away from the subject or postpone it. Her daughter had never seen her so deeply in earnest, so intent upon having her way, before. On previous occasions it had been Hester that had won the day. But this time the girl had to give way to the impassioned earnestness of her mother, which in so mild a woman was strange to see.

CHAPTER XIV
THE PARTY AT THE GRANGE

Catherine's Christmas party called forth all Redborough. It was an assembly to which the best people in the place considered themselves bound to go, notwithstanding that many of the small people were there also. Everybody indeed was supposed to come, and all classes were represented. The respectable old clerks, who had spent their lives in the bank, talked upon equal terms, according to the fiction of society, with the magnates of the town, and Edward and Harry Vernon, and others of the golden youth, asked their daughters to dance. The great ladies in their jewels sat about upon the sofas, and so did Mrs. Halifax, the cashier's wife, and Mrs. Brown, the head clerk's, in their ribbons. All was supposed to be equality and happiness; if it were not so, then the fault was upon the shoulders of the guests, and not of the hostess, who walked about from one to another, and was so civil to Mrs. Brown—so very civil—that Lady Freemantle could not help whispering to Mrs. Merridew that, after all, when a woman had once been engaged in business, it always left a mark upon her.

"She is more at home with those sort of persons than she is with the county," Lady Freemantle said.

Mrs. Merridew was deeply flattered with the confidence, and gave a most cordial assent. "It does give a sort of an unfeminine turn of mind, though dear Miss Vernon is so universally respected," she said.

This little dialogue would have given Catherine sincere enjoyment if she had heard it. She divined it from the conjunction of Lady Freemantle's diamonds with Mrs. Merridew's lace, as they leant towards each other, and from the expression and direction of their eyes.

On her side Mrs. Brown drew conclusions quite as fallacious. "Miss Vernon is well aware how much the young gentlemen owe to Brown," that lady said afterwards, "and how devoted he is. She knows his value to the business, and I am sure she sees that a share in the bank is what he has a right to look to."

This delusion, however, Catherine did not divine.

It was with a reluctance and repugnance indescribable that Hester had come: but she was there, by the side of her mother, who, a little alarmed by the crowd, did not know what to do with herself, until Harry Vernon interposed and led her to the corner of a sofa, in the very midst of the fine people, which poor Mrs. John, divided between the pride which was too proud to take a chief place and the consciousness that this place was her right, hesitated greatly upon.

"I think I should like to be farther off," she said, faltering; "down there somewhere," and she pointed in the direction of the Mrs. Browns—"or anywhere," she added, getting confused.

"This is your proper place," said Harry out of his moustache, with persistence.

The poor lady sat down in a nervous flutter in her black silk gown, which looked very nice, but had lasted a long time, and though it had been kept, so to speak, within sight of the fashion by frequent alterations, was very different from the elegant mixture of velvet and satin, fresh from the hands of a court milliner, which swept over the greater part of the space. Mrs. John had a little cap made of a piece of fine Mechlin upon her hair, which was still very pretty, and of the dark brown satin kind. Her ornaments were of the most modest description, whereas the other lady had a set of emeralds which were the admiration of the county. Hester stood behind her mother very erect and proud, in her white muslin, with her pearls, looking like a maid of honour to a mild, discrowned queen. A maid of honour in such circumstances would stand a great deal more upon her dignity than her mistress would be likely to do. This was the aspect they presented to the lookers-on who saw them in that unusual eminence. When Catherine perceived where her poor pensioners were placed, she gave way to a momentary impatience.

"Who put Mrs. John there?" she said to Edward, almost with anger. "Don't you see how thoroughly out of place she looks? You may think it shows a fine regard for the fallen, but she would have been much more comfortable at the other end among the people she knows."

"I had nothing to do with it. I have not spoken to them," said Edward with a certain sullenness. He was glad to be able to exculpate himself, and yet he despised himself all the more fiercely.

Catherine was vexed in a way which she herself felt to be unworthy, but which she said to herself was entirely justified by the awkwardness of the situation.

"I suppose it is Harry that has done it," she said, her voice softened by the discovery that Edward at least was not to blame. "It must be said for him, at least, that he is very faithful to his family."

Did she mean that *he* was not faithful? Edward asked himself. Did even she despise him? But he could not now change his course, or stoop to follow Harry's example, that oaf who was inaccessible to the fluctuations of sentiment around him, and could do nothing but cling to his one idea. It cannot be said, however, that either Mrs. John or Hester were at their ease in their present position. It was true, as Catherine had said, that with the curate's wife Mrs. John would have been much more comfortable, and this consciousness wounded the poor lady, who felt now she was out of place among the people to whom she was allied by nature. She was accustomed to the slight of being put in a lower place, but to feel herself so completely out of her old position, went to her heart. She looked timidly, poor soul, at the great lady with the emeralds, remembering when she, too, used to be in the order of great ladies, and wondering if in those days she had ever despised the lowly. But when she thus raised her eyes she found that the lady of the emeralds was looking very fixedly at her.

"Surely," she said, after a little hesitation, "this must be Lucy Westwood."

"Yes," said Mrs. John wistfully, investigating the stranger with her timid eyes.

"Then have you forgotten 'Bridget—Fidget'?" said the other.

It was a school name, and it brought a glow upon Mrs. John's pale face. An old school-fellow! She forgot all the painful past and her present embarrassment, and even her daughter. Hester stood for some time in her maid-of-honour attitude and contemplated the conversation. She heard her mother say, "This is my girl—the only one I have," and felt herself crimsoning and curtseying vaguely to some one she scarcely saw; then the stranger added—

"I have three here; but I think they are all dancing."

Yes, no doubt there was dancing going on, but Hester had no part in it. She became tired, after a while, of her post of maid of honour. Her wonderful indignant carriage, the poise of her young head, the proud air of independence which was evident in her, called forth the admiration of many of the spectators. "Who is that girl?" said the elder people, who only came once a year, and were unacquainted with the gossip of Redborough. "John Vernon's daughter? Oh, that was the man who ought to have married Catherine—he who nearly ruined the bank. And that is her mother? How good of Catherine to have them here." If Hester had heard these remarks she would have had few questions to ask about her father. But she was unaware of the notice she was attracting, placed thus at the head of the great drawing-room. The folding doors had been removed and the two rooms made into one. The girl was in the most conspicuous position without knowing; her white figure stood out against the wall, with her little mother in the foreground. She stood for a long time looking out with large eyes, full of light, upon the crowd, her varying emotions very legible in her face. When a creature so young and full of life feels herself neglected and disdained, and sees others about her whom her keen eyes cannot help but see are inferior to herself, promoted far above her, enjoying what is forbidden to her, finding pleasure where she has none—yet is bound to the spot and cannot escape, it is natural that indignation should light fires in her eyes, and that her breast should swell and her young countenance glow with a visionary scorn of all who seem to scorn her. This sentiment is neither amiable nor desirable, but it gave a sort of inspiration to Hester—her head so erect, slightly thrown back, her nostrils a little dilated, her mouth shut close, her eyes large and open, regarding in full face the world of enemies against whom, wholly or singly, she felt herself ready to stand. All this gave a character and individuality to her such as nothing in the room could equal. But by and by she tired of standing, shut out from everybody, holding up her banner. She stole away from her mother's side, behind the chairs, to get to somebody she knew and could talk to. Flesh and blood cannot bear this sort of martyrdom of pride for ever.

An old man was standing in her way, who made a little movement to stop Hester as she passed. "You will excuse an old friend, Miss Hester," he said; "but I must tell you how glad I am to see you and your mother. I have been looking at you both ever since you came. She is very much changed since I used to see her, but her sweet expression is the same. That is a thing that will never change."

"I think I know you," said Hester, with the shy frankness which was so unlike her hostile attitude. "Did not I see you at Captain Morgan's? and you said something to me about my mother?"

"I had not much time to tell you then. I should just like to describe it to you," said the old clerk. "I have never forgotten that day. I was in a dreadful state of anxiety, fearing that everything was coming to an end; and the only place I could think of going to was the White House. That was where your parents were staying at the time. No, no, they were not your parents then; I think there was a little baby that died— —"

"I was born abroad," said Hester, eager to catch every word.

"Yes, yes, to be sure; and she was quite young, not much older than you are now. It was in that long room at the White House, with a window at each end, which is the dining-room now. You will excuse me for being a little long-winded, Miss Hester. It was beautifully furnished, as we thought then; and there was a harp and a piano. Does your mamma ever play the harp now? No, no, I ought to remember, that has quite gone out of fashion. She had her hair high up on her head like this," said Mr. Rule, trying to give a pantomimic description on the top of his own grey head of the high bows which had once adorned Mrs. John's. "She had a white dress on, far shorter than you wear them now; and little slippers with crossed bands, sandals they used to call them. Oh, I remember everything like a picture! Ladies used to wear little short sleeves in those days, and low dresses. She had a little scarf round her over one shoulder. What a pretty creature she was, to be sure! I had been so wretched and anxious that the sight of her as I came rushing in, had the strangest effect upon me. All bank business and our troubles about money, and the terror of a run, which was what I was frightened for, seemed nothing but ugly dreams, without any reality in them. I dare say you don't know, Miss Hester, what I mean by a run?"

"No, indeed," said Hester, a little impatient; "but I should like to know what happened after."

"A run on the bank," said the old clerk, "is the most terrible thing in all creation. A battle is nothing to it—for in a battle you can at least fight for your life. It happens when the partners or the company, or whatever they may be, have had losses, or are reported to have had losses, and a rumour gets up against the bank. Sometimes it may be a long time threatening, sometimes it may get up in a single day—but as soon as the rumour gets the length of a panic, everybody that has money deposited comes to draw it out, and everybody that has a note of the bank comes for his money. In those days Vernon's issued notes, like all the other great country banks. I was in mortal terror for a run: I never was in such a state in my life. And it was then, as I told you, Miss Hester, that I went to your mother. Of course we had not money enough to meet it—the most solvent could scarcely hope to have that at a moment's notice. Next day was the market day, and I knew that, as sure as life— —! I have passed through many a troublesome moment, but never one like that."

And, as if even the thinking of it was more than he could bear, the old clerk took out his handkerchief and wiped his forehead. Hester had listened with great interest, but still with a little impatience: for though the run upon the bank would have interested her at another time, it was more than her attention was equal to now.

"But was not my father here as well as my mother?" said Hester, in her clear voice, unconscious of any need to subdue it.

Mr. Rule looked at her with a startled air and a half-involuntary "Hush!"

"Your father!" he said, with a tone of consternation. "Oh; the fact was that your father—did not happen to be there at the time."

Hester waved her hand slightly as a token for him to go on. She had a feeling that these words were of more importance than they seemed to be, but they confused her, and she did not as yet see what this importance was. She remembered that she had thought so when he told her this incident before.

"Where was I?" said Mr. Rule. "Oh, yes, I remember; just going into the White House with my mind full of trouble, not knowing what to do. Well, Miss Hester, when I found that your—I mean when I discovered that your—mother was alone, I told her the dreadful condition I was in—Nobody to say what to do, no chief authority to direct, and market-day to-morrow, and a run as sure as fate. Now, you know, we could have telegraphed all over the country, but there was no such thing as a telegraph then. I had to explain it to her just as I have to you, and I feel sure she didn't understand me in the very least. She only knew there was money wanted. She stepped across the room in her pretty sandals, with her scarf hanging from her shoulders, as if she had been going to play her harp, and opened a little bit of a desk, one of those gimcrack things, all rosewood and velvet, which were the fashion then, and took out all her money and brought it to me. It was in our own notes, poor dear," said old Rule, with a little laugh; "and it came to just twenty pounds. She would have made me take it—forced it upon me. She did not understand a bit. She was full of trouble and sympathy, and ready to give up everything. Ah, I have often told Miss Vernon since. It was not want of will; it was only that she did not understand."

"I am sure you mean to speak kindly of mamma," said Hester, with a quick blush of alarmed pride; "but I don't think it is so difficult to make her understand. And what did you do after that? Was there a run—and how did you provide—?"

She did not know what to say, the questions seemed to get into her throat and choke her. There was something else which she could not understand which must soon be made clear. She gave furtive glances at the old clerk, but did not look him in the face.

"Ah, I went to Miss Vernon. She was but a young lady then. Oh, I don't mean to say young like you. It is thirty years ago. She was older than your pretty young mamma, and though she had a great share in the business she never had taken any part in it. But she was come of a family that have all had fine heads for business. Look at Mr. Edward now: what a clear understanding he has, and sees exactly the right thing to do, whatever happens. She was a little shocked and startled just at first, but she took it up in a moment, no man could have done it better. She signed away all her money in the twinkling of an eye, and saved the bank. When all the crowd of the country folk came rushing to draw out their money, she stepped in—well, like a kind of goddess to us, Miss Hester—and paid in almost her whole fortune, all her mother's money, every penny she had out of the business, and pulled us through. I can remember her too, as if it had been yesterday, the way she stepped in—with her head held high, and a kind of a triumph about her; something like what I have seen in yourself, my dear young lady."

"Seen in me! You have never seen me with any triumph about me," cried Hester, bitterly. "And where have you seen me? I scarcely know you. Ah, that was because of the money she had. My mother, with her twenty pounds, what could she do? But Catherine was rich. It was because of her money."

"Her money was a great deal: but it was not the money alone. It was the heart and the courage she had. We had nobody to tell us what to do—but after she came, all went well. She had such a head for business."

Hester could not stand and listen to Catherine's praises; but she was entirely absorbed in the narrative. It seemed terrible to her that she had not been there to be able to step in as Catherine had done. But there was another question pressing upon her which she had asked already, and to which she had got no reply. She shrank from repeating it yet felt a force upon her to do so. She fixed her large widely-opened eyes upon the speaker, so as to lose none of the indications of his face.

"Will you tell me," she said, "how it was that you had, as you say, nobody to tell you anything—no one at the head—nobody to say what was to be done?"

Old Mr. Rule did not immediately reply. He made a little pause, and shuffled with his feet, looking down at them, not meeting her eyes.

"Hester," said Ellen Merridew, who was passing, and paused on her partner's arm to interfere, "why don't you dance? What do you mean by not dancing? What are you doing here behind backs? I have been looking for you everywhere."

"I prefer to be here," Hester answered, shortly; "never mind me, please. Mr. Rule, will you answer me? I want to know."

"You asked how it was that we— — What was it you asked, Miss Hester? I am very glad to see you so interested: but you ought to be dancing, not talking to an old man, as Mrs. Merridew says."

"I think you are all in a plot against me," said Hester, impatiently; "why was it you were left without a head? What had happened? Mr. Rule," cried the girl, "you know what I asked, and you know why I am so anxious. You are trying to put me off. What does it all mean?"

"It is an old story," he said; "I cannot tell what tempted me to begin about it. It was seeing you and your mother for the first time. You were not at Miss Vernon's party last year?"

"What has that to do with it?" cried Hester. "If you will not tell me, say so. I shall find out some other way."

"My dear young lady, ask me anything. Don't find out any other way. I will come and see you, if your mamma will permit me, and tell you everything about the old days. But I can't keep you longer now. And, besides, it would need a great deal of explanation. I was foolish to begin about it here, keeping you out of your natural amusement. But I'll come and tell you, Miss Hester, with pleasure," said the old man, putting on a show of easy cordiality, "any day you will name."

"Hester," said another voice over her head, "Ellen says I am not to let you stay here. Come and see the supper-room. And the hall is very pretty. I am not to go without you, Ellen says."

"Oh, what do I care for Ellen!" cried Hester, exasperated. "Go away, Harry; go and dance and amuse yourself. I don't want you or any one. Mr. Rule— —"

But the old clerk had seized his opportunity. He had made a dart at some one else on the other side while Hester turned to reply to Harry's demand. The girl found herself abandoned when she turned to him again. There had been a gradual shifting in the groups about while she stood absorbed listening to his story. She was standing now among people who were strange to her, and who looked at her curiously, knowing her to be "one of the family." As she met their curious eyes, Hester, though she had a high courage, felt her heart fail her. She was glad to fall back upon her cousin's support.

"I think you are all in a conspiracy against me," she said; but she took Harry's arm. He never abandoned her in any circumstances. Edward had not spoken to her, nor noticed her presence; but Harry never failed. In her excitement and disappointment she turned to him with a sense that here she could not go wrong. As for Harry, to whom she was seldom so complacent, he drew her arm within his own with a flush of pleasure.

"I know you don't think much of me," he said, "but surely I am as good as that old fellow!" a speech at which Hester could not but laugh. "I should like to know what he was saying to you," Harry said.

"He was telling me about the run on the bank and how Catherine saved it. Do you know—I wonder—— Had my father never anything to do with it?" Hester said.

They were making their way through the crowd at the end of the room. And Harry's countenance was not expressive. Hester thought the stare in his eyes was directed to somebody behind who had pushed against her. She was not suspicious that Harry could hide from her any knowledge he possessed.

"That was ages before my time," he said very steadily. "You might as well ask me about the flood;" and so led her on through the many groups about the door, entirely unsuspicious that he, too, for whom she had an affectionate contempt, had baulked her. She allowed him to take her over all the lighted rooms which opened into each other: the hall, the library, the room blazing with lights and decorations, which was prepared for supper. Hester had never been before at one of these great assemblies. And she could not keep herself entirely unmoved by the dazzling of the lights, the warmth and largeness of the entertainment. A sort of pride came upon her, surprising her in spite of herself: though she was so humble a member of the family, and subject under this roof to slights and scorns, yet she was a Vernon, and could not escape some reflection of the family glory which centred in Catherine. And as she went into the hall a still more strange sensation suddenly came over Hester. She caught sight, in a large mirror, of herself stepping forward, her head held high in its habitual poise of half indignant energy, and a certain swiftness in her air and movement, a sentiment of forward motion and progress, very familiar to everybody who knew her, but which brought suddenly to her mind old Rule's description, "stepping in with a kind of triumph about her, as I have seen yourself." "Triumph!" Hester said secretly within herself, and coloured high, with a sensation of mingled pain and pleasure, which no words could have described. She did not know what it meant; but it stirred her strangely. If she had been in these circumstances she would have acted like Catherine. The story of her mother in her gentle ignorance, which the old clerk thought so much of, did not affect the high-spirited girl as did the picture of the other putting herself in the breach, taking upon her own shoulders the weight of the falling house. Hester felt that she, too, could have done this. Her breast swelled, her breath came short with an impulse of impatience and longing to have such an opportunity, to show the mettle that was in her. But how could she do it? Catherine was rich, but Hester was poor. In this way she was diverted for the moment from her anxiety. The question as to how the bank came into that peril, the suspicion that her father must have been somehow connected with it, the heat of her research after the key of the mystery, faded away for the moment in a vague, general excitement and eager yet vain desire to have it in her power to do something, she also——a desire which many a young mind has felt as well as Hester; to have that golden opportunity—the occasion to do a heroic deed, to save some one, to venture your own life, to escape the bonds of every day, and once have a chance of showing what was in you! This was not the "chance" which Emma Ashton desired, but it appealed to every sentiment in Hester. The strong longing for it seemed almost to promise a possibility, as she walked along in a dream, without noticing Harry by her side. And he did not disturb her by conversation. It was enough for Harry to feel her hand on his arm. He had never very much to say, and he did not insist upon saying it. He was content to lead her about, to show her everything; and the sensation of taking care of her was pleasant to his heart.

When they reached the hall, however, they became aware of a late arrival, which had a certain effect upon both. Standing near the great door, which had been opened a minute before to admit him, sending a thrill of cold night air through the whole warm succession of rooms, stood Roland Ashton. Hester was aware that he was expected, but not that he was coming here. A servant was helping him off with his coat, and Edward stood beside him in eager conversation. Edward's countenance, generally toned down to the air of decorum and self-command which he thought necessary, was excited and glowing. And Harry, too, lighted up when he saw the new comer. "Ah, there's Ashton!" he said; while from one of the other doors Catherine Vernon herself, with a white shawl over her shoulders, came out from amidst her other guests to welcome her kinsman. It was a wonderful reception for a young man who was not distinguished either by rank or wealth. Hester had to hang back, keeping persistently in the shade, to prevent her companion from hurrying forward into the circle of welcoming faces.

"I felt the cold air from the door at the very end of the drawing-room," Catherine said; "but though it made me shiver it was not unwelcome, Roland. I knew that it meant that you had come."

"I wish my coming had not cost you a shiver," Roland cried.

"One moment; I must say how d'ye do to him," said Harry in Hester's ear; and even he, the faithfulest one, left her for a moment to hold out his hand to the new comer.

The girl stood apart, sheltering herself under the shade of the plants with which the hall was filled, and looked on at this scene. There was in the whole group a curious connection with herself. Even to Catherine she, perhaps, poor girl as she was, was the guest among all the others who roused the keenest feeling. Edward, who did not venture to look at her here, had given her every reason to believe that his mind was full of her. Harry had put his life at her disposal. Roland—Roland had taken possession of her mind and thoughts for a few weeks with a completeness of influence which probably he never intended, which, perhaps, was nothing at all to him, which it made Hester blush to remember. They all stood together, their faces lighted up with interest while she looked on. Hester stood under a great myrtle bush, which shaded her face, and looked at them in the thrill of the excitement which the previous events of the evening had called forth. A sort of prophetic sense that the lives of all were linked with her own, a presentiment that between them and among them it would be hers to work either for weal or woe, came over her like a sudden revelation. It was altogether fanciful and absurd she felt; but the impression was so strong that she turned and fled, with a sudden impulse to avoid the fate that seemed almost to overshadow her as she stood and looked at them. She, who a moment before had been longing for the heroic opportunity, the power of interposing as Catherine had interposed, felt all the panic of a child come over her as she stood and gazed at the four people, not one of whom was indifferent to her. She hurried out of the comparative quiet of the hall into the crowd, and made her way with a trembling of nervous excitement to where her mother sat. Mrs. John was still seated serenely on her sofa talking of old school-days and comrades with the lady of the emeralds. She was serene, yet there was a little gentle excitement about her too, a little additional colour upon her soft cheek. Hester, with her heart beating loudly and a strange tumult in her veins, took refuge behind her mother with a sense of protection which she had never felt before. The soft nature which was ready to be touched by any gentle emotion, which understood none of life's problems, yet, by patience and simplicity, sailed over them all, is often a shield to those that see more and feel more. Behind her unconscious mother Hester seemed to herself to take refuge from her fate.

It was a great elevation to Mrs. John to sit there at the upper part of the room, among the great ladies, out of the crowd of less distinguished persons. Her feeling of embarrassed shyness and sense of being out of place had all vanished when she discovered her old friend; and from that time she had begun to enjoy herself with a soothing consciousness that all proper respect was paid to her, and that at last, without any doing of hers, all, as she said to herself, had come right. She assented with gentle cordiality to all that was said to her about the beauty of the house, and the perfection of the arrangements.

"Catherine is wonderful," she said; "she has such a head; she understands everything," and not a feeling in her heart contradicted her words.

That evening was, in its way, a gentle triumph to the gentle little woman. Hester had disappeared from her for a time, and had been, she had no doubt, enjoying herself; and then she had come back and stood dutifully by her mother, such a maid of honour as any queen might have been proud of. She had a thousand things to say of the assembly; of dear Bridget Wilton, who recollected her so well, and who was now quite a great person; of the prettiness of the party, and the girls' dresses, and all the light and brilliancy of the scene—when at last it was all over and they had reached home.

"Now I am sure you are glad you went," she said, with innocent confidence. "It is a long, long time since I have spent so pleasant an evening. You see Catherine would not allow me to be overlooked when it was really a great party. She knows very well what is due. She did not mind at those little evenings, which are of no importance; but to-night you could see how different it was. Bridget insisted that Sir John himself should take me to supper. No, dear, it was nothing more than was right, but it shows, what I always thought, that no neglect was ever intended. And Catherine was very kind. I am sure now you are glad you went."

Was she glad she had gone? Hester could not tell. She closed the door between her and her mother as if she were afraid that Mrs. John in her unusual exhilaration might read her thoughts. These thoughts were almost too great to be confined within her own spirit. As she lay down in the dark she seemed to see the light shining all about her, the groups in the ball-room—the old man garrulous, deep in the revelations of the past, and the cluster of figures all standing together under the light of the lamps, exchanging questions which meant, though she could scarcely tell how, the future to Hester. Perhaps, on the whole, it was true, and she was glad she had gone.